A CHANCE FALL

(THE INN AT DUNE ISLAND—BOOK 2)

FIONA GRACE

Fiona Grace

Fiona Grace is author of the LACEY DOYLE COZY MYSTERY series, comprising nine books; of the TUSCAN VINEYARD COZY MYSTERY series, comprising seven books; of the DUBIOUS WITCH COZY MYSTERY series, comprising three books; of the BEACHFRONT BAKERY COZY MYSTERY series, comprising six books; of the CATS AND DOGS COZY MYSTERY series, comprising nine books; of the ELIZA MONTAGU COZY MYSTERY series, comprising nine books (and counting); of the ENDLESS HARBOR ROMANTIC COMEDY series, comprising nine books (and counting); of the INN AT DUNE ISLAND ROMANTIC COMEDY series, comprising five books (and counting); of the INN BY THE SEA ROMANTIC COMEDY series, comprising five books (and counting); and of the MAID AND THE MANSION COZY MYSTERY series, comprising five books (and counting).

Fiona would love to hear from you, so please visit www.fionagraceauthor.com to receive free ebooks, hear the latest news, and stay in touch.

A SPEAKEASY DEMISE (Book #4)
A FLAPPER FATALITY (Book #5)
BUMPED BY A DAME (Book #6)
A DOLL'S DEBACLE (Book #7)
A FELLA'S RUIN (Book #8)
A GAL'S OFFING (Book #9)

LACEY DOYLE COZY MYSTERY
MURDER IN THE MANOR (Book#1)
DEATH AND A DOG (Book #2)
CRIME IN THE CAFE (Book #3)
VEXED ON A VISIT (Book #4)
KILLED WITH A KISS (Book #5)
PERISHED BY A PAINTING (Book #6)
SILENCED BY A SPELL (Book #7)
FRAMED BY A FORGERY (Book #8)
CATASTROPHE IN A CLOISTER (Book #9)

TUSCAN VINEYARD COZY MYSTERY
AGED FOR MURDER (Book #1)
AGED FOR DEATH (Book #2)
AGED FOR MAYHEM (Book #3)
AGED FOR SEDUCTION (Book #4)
AGED FOR VENGEANCE (Book #5)
AGED FOR ACRIMONY (Book #6)
AGED FOR MALICE (Book #7)

DUBIOUS WITCH COZY MYSTERY
SKEPTIC IN SALEM: AN EPISODE OF MURDER (Book #1)
SKEPTIC IN SALEM: AN EPISODE OF CRIME (Book #2)
SKEPTIC IN SALEM: AN EPISODE OF DEATH (Book #3)

BEACHFRONT BAKERY COZY MYSTERY
BEACHFRONT BAKERY: A KILLER CUPCAKE (Book #1)
BEACHFRONT BAKERY: A MURDEROUS MACARON (Book #2)
BEACHFRONT BAKERY: A PERILOUS CAKE POP (Book #3)
BEACHFRONT BAKERY: A DEADLY DANISH (Book #4)
BEACHFRONT BAKERY: A TREACHEROUS TART (Book #5)
BEACHFRONT BAKERY: A CALAMITOUS COOKIE (Book #6)

CATS AND DOGS COZY MYSTERY
A VILLA IN SICILY: OLIVE OIL AND MURDER (Book #1)
A VILLA IN SICILY: FIGS AND A CADAVER (Book #2)
A VILLA IN SICILY: VINO AND DEATH (Book #3)
A VILLA IN SICILY: CAPERS AND CALAMITY (Book #4)
A VILLA IN SICILY: ORANGE GROVES AND VENGEANCE
(Book #5)
A VILLA IN SICILY: CANNOLI AND A CASUALTY (Book #6)

CHAPTER ONE

Windows had yet to begin fogging up from the chill of the fall weather. Outside, the leaves fell quickly off of the tall trees as April watched from inside Nigel's home. She took another sip of her tea, closed her eyes and smiled.

"Dinner is served," Nigel said from the doorway that led to the kitchen.

He laid out a delicious spread across the table. Roasted vegetables, steak, garlic and herb potatoes. It was a regal meal that made April thankful she was dating a chef.

It was only their third date, in part because April had been so busy with the renovations on the bed and breakfast. But she knew that there was something special here.

Thankfully, the bed and breakfast she'd made out of her childhood vacation home was getting somewhere. Two rooms were complete, along with most of the common spaces. They were already booked for her soft opening tomorrow.

"This looks delicious," April said, beginning to serve herself portions of the steaming dishes. "Thank you for making dinner. I'm sure it's not fun to bring work home with you."

"Oh, please. I love my job. Happy to cook for you any day." His smile gave her butterflies. "How are you feeling about the first guests coming tomorrow?"

Honestly, she was terrified.

She'd been waiting for this moment for so long, and now it was finally here. Her life had revolved around this house for months. All of her dreams lay in the success of that place.

There was still work to be done for the other rooms to become available. But the soft open was a huge deal. It meant that people were finally coming. Real customers, real people with real opinions.

April took a deep breath.

"I'm nervous, but excited. I just want everything to go smoothly."

Nigel reached across the table and took her hand. "Don't worry, April. You've put so much hard work into this place, and it shows. Your guests will love it."

1

April smiled, feeling reassured by Nigel's words. She couldn't believe how lucky she was to have someone like him in her life.

Nigel continued, "You deserve this success."

She felt a warmth spread through her chest as she squeezed his hand. She knew he was right. She had poured her heart and soul into this bed and breakfast, and it was finally paying off.

Rising to his feet, Nigel stepped closer to her, still hand in hand. He placed his other hand on top of hers. He got down on a knee to look her in the eye. "I'm really thankful to have met you," he said.

April's cheeks grew hot, unable to contain her excitement. "I'm glad I met you too."

Nigel's face slowly got closer to hers. She looked down at his lips, ready for their first kiss. She'd been waiting for this moment since the day she met him.

And just when their lips were about to touch, a knock came at the door.

"One second," Nigel said, standing to get it. His face fell, disappointed. "Just don't forget where we left off."

She wouldn't. She couldn't.

April smiled at him. She took another sip of her tea. Who could possibly be showing up in the middle of their date? Nigel's restaurant was being run by his workers. Maybe there was an emergency.

"Hello, Nigel," April heard from the front door. A woman's voice, low and sultry.

April's heart dropped. Who was this woman at Nigel's door? She turned to find Nigel staring at a gorgeous, tall woman in a tight dress and black heels.

"Lily, what are you doing here? I thought you'd moved away."

April felt a knot form in her stomach as she watched Nigel and Lily greet each other with a hug. She didn't like the way Lily was looking at Nigel, as if there was some sort of history between them.

"I did, but I'm back in town," Lily said, her eyes flickering over to April. "I'm sorry, I didn't realize you had company."

Nigel turned to April, a look of apology on his face. "April, this is Lily. An old friend."

April forced a smile and stood up to greet Lily. "Nice to meet you, Lily."

Lily gave her a curt nod before turning back to Nigel. "I was hoping we could catch up. Maybe grab a drink?"

2

Nigel hesitated, glancing over at April. "Actually, I'm in the middle of something right now. Maybe another time?"

Lily looked disappointed but nodded. "Sure, I understand. Just let me know."

As she walked out the door, April couldn't shake the feeling that there was more to their relationship than just old friends catching up. Nigel had never mentioned Lily before, and the way they had hugged and looked at each other was anything but platonic.

"Nigel, who was that?" April asked.

When he came back to the table, he didn't resume where they'd left off. He sat back in his chair across from her. "That was Lily. She's uh... my ex-girlfriend."

April wasn't so sure Lily was an ex, based on how they spoke. After all, this was only their third date. How long ago had he been dating that beautiful woman, begging for his attention.

"And she's back in town?"

He looked around the room, unable to meet her eyes or continue his dinner. "I guess so. I had no idea she was coming. Or that she would come here."

"It seems as though the two of you have a lot to talk about."

April tried to stop her eyes from watering, but there was nothing she could do. A tear fell down her cheek.

Nigel shook his head and finally looked her in the eye. "No, no. That's not what's happening here. I want to be with you. I just..."

"Just wasn't expecting the love of your life to walk back to your door. I get it."

April pushed her chair back, stood up, and wiped the tears from her eyes. She couldn't believe she was getting emotional over a man she'd only been dating for a few weeks.

"I think I should go," she said, grabbing her coat and purse. "I need some time to think."

Nigel stood up too, his eyes pleading with her not to leave. "April, please. Don't go. We can talk about this. Or we can forget about it and continue our date."

"I can't just forget about it. You have some things to sort out, Nigel. I don't want to be in the middle of it."

"April, please don't go. This isn't what you think it is. I'm just... thinking. Don't let this get between us." His eyes begged her to stay, but she knew she couldn't.

She was so confused. The night didn't go as she expected it to. She couldn't decipher Nigel's thoughts. And that scared her.

April grabbed her coat and headed for the door. She heard him call her name, but she didn't turn back.

Outside, the air was freezing cold. A chill ran down her spine as she walked to her car. She wanted to get as far away from Nigel's house as possible.

The thought of facing guests the next day made her stomach sick. It wasn't just that she was nervous about guests, but now she didn't want to face Nigel, who would no doubt be making an appearance.

As she drove home, she tried not to think about how tomorrow was going to be one of the hardest days of her life.

CHAPTER TWO

April woke to the sound of her alarm. As soon as she turned it off, she was replaying the events of last night in her head.

Nigel's ex-girlfriend was back in town and clearly wanted to see him again. And Nigel didn't seem too keen to let Lily know that they were on their third date.

Did Nigel really want to be with April? Or was she just a second choice to the woman who left town?

Her chest felt heavy as she sat up in bed, dreading the day ahead of her. The bed and breakfast still needed some last-minute touches. That was what she should be focusing on.

The first two guests were checking in today. It should have been a joyful yet nerve-racking morning. But all she felt was anxiety.

As April began to tidy up the first floor of the house, she called Georgia. It was her daughter's first day back at school after leaving suddenly last semester.

It took her helping with turning the old family home into a bed and breakfast to get her interested in going back. And this time, she was actually pursuing something she wanted to do forever, interior design.

"Hey, mom," Georgia said as she answered.

April smiled at the sound of her daughter's voice, grateful for the distraction. "Good morning, sweetheart. How was your first day back?"

"It was great, actually," Georgia replied with a hint of excitement. "I got to meet some of the other interior design students, and they all seem really cool. Plus, my professor seems super chill."

April's smile widened, glad to hear that her daughter was enjoying her time back at school. "That's wonderful, sweetie. I'm so proud of you."

"Thanks, mom," Georgia said with a sigh. "How's the first day prep coming along?"

When she paused, her daughter became suspicious. "What's going on? You okay? Do you need me to come down there?"

"No," April exclaimed quickly. "I just mean... It's your first day. You're not coming down here just because I'm a little bit overwhelmed.

It's my first guests coming in today. I'm bound to be nervous. It'll be okay."

"Alright, if you say so. Listen, I hate to cut this short, but I have to get to my next class. I'll call you later, okay?"

She felt the ball in her stomach tighten back up again. "Of course, love you," April replied before hanging up.

Though she was hoping for a longer call, April felt a sense of pride wash over her. She was so happy that her daughter had found her passion and was pursuing it with such enthusiasm.

April continued with her last-minute prep. This was the last time she was going to see this place as her home, and the first time she would see it as her bed and breakfast.

She walked around the house, checking in on the details she'd worked so hard to create. The large doors at the front of the house sat open and wide for everyone to see into the lobby, what used to be the living room.

The front desk that sat in the entryway was polished and gleaming. The rooms upstairs were all cleaned and ready for guests, and the smell of fresh coffee wafted through the air from the kitchen.

April took a deep breath and reminded herself that she was ready for this. She had put her heart and soul into this bed and breakfast, and it was going to show.

She heard the sound of a car pulling up outside and quickly checked her watch. It was almost time for her first guests to arrive. Her nerves started to resurface as she took a deep breath and walked towards the front door.

Two people stepped out of the sleek black car. The man wore cargo shorts and a floral button-up. If April had looked up a picture of a male tourist, she thought that he would be what showed up. She giggled silently at his goofy smile.

The short woman had kind eyes, blue and full of wonder. Together, they looked over the property, smiling and staring out at the ocean from the hilltop.

April was glad that even the placement of the home was perfect. After checking in, her guests would be able to go down to that private beach and enjoy the water and sand.

But for now, they stood at the edge of the stairs, looking down at the waves. The man got out a camera and began to snap pictures of the adorable woman, posing for him as if a model in a photoshoot.

This was exactly why she built this place.

For people like them to come and enjoy Sandcrest, the beautiful town she'd always loved growing up. April had been dreaming of this moment since she stepped back onto the island.

Her dream for the bed and breakfast was to create a place for tourists and residents to enjoy their time on the island. This was what it was made for.

Yet she couldn't help but look on with fear in her heart as she witnessed the happy couple enjoying their vacation.

She watched them giggle, the wife's head nuzzled into her husband's chest. The only care they had was watching the shoreline as the waves curved and swallowed the beach.

April couldn't shake off the memories of her ex-husband, who had left her to travel the world. Though he was probably on his world tour of circuses and not looking over a beach with contemplation in his eyes.

Seeing happy couples like this made her question everything. Her past and her present. Because Nigel clearly wasn't in the best place for her either.

She cursed herself for letting the thoughts of Nigel and his ex-girlfriend invade her mind. She was a strong woman who had worked hard to get where she was. And now it was finally time to show it off.

April needed to focus on her soft launch. Those people looking over the hill and taking in the view, they should be her focus.

As the couple began to walk towards the door, hand in hand, a sound got April's attention. Another car was speeding down her driveway.

She assumed it must be the other guest, though she wondered why they would be going so fast when it specifically said on the welcome instructions to go slow down the drive.

Hopefully, they wouldn't be ignoring all of her other rules for the stay. Like don't drive on the grass, walk carefully down the steps to the beach and no parties without approval.

Even the couple turned to look at the screeching car. They looked over at April. "Sorry, I'm sure they just forgot to read the travel instructions," she reassured them.

They smiled back at her, but their expressions looked full of pity more than anything else.

April welcomed them into the lobby with wide open arms and then slid past them to step into the driveway. She wanted to remind the next guest that there were wild animals around, children, people walking the streets.

The island was supposed to be a place of quiet beaches, not revving engines.

As she walked down the driveway, April could feel her heart begin to race. The sound of the car grew louder and louder, and she wondered who could be driving so recklessly.

The car screeched to a stop in front of her, kicking up dust and small rocks. The driver side door opened and a tall, broad-shouldered man stepped out.

"Excuse me," she said with a fake smile. April opened her mouth to talk again, but was silenced by the man getting out of the driver's side door. Something about him caught her attention.

His suit was tailored, but from years ago the shirt pressed against his chest tightly. The sandy brown hair was familiar, but of something from her past.

It wasn't until she examined the man's face that she finally realized who she was staring at.

The wrinkles were new, along with the wear on his rough hands. She realized now why the hair was so familiar. It was in the style she knew, but sparkled with slivers of gray hair.

"Dad?"

The man looked up at her with a sly grin. "April. Good to see you."

CHAPTER THREE

"Dad, what are you doing here?"

He looked April up and down, something April hated. She didn't want him making any assumptions about her. In fact, she didn't want her father thinking about her at all.

With a smile, her father replied, "I'm happy to see you, too." He put out his arms to hug her. Unsure of what to do, she allowed him to come in, but weakly wrapped her arms around his shoulders.

They stepped apart, and April felt her heart begin to race. After seeing his daughter's uneasy expression, Richard said, "I heard you were updating the 'ole place. I wanted to see it again."

He looked up at the house, taking in all of its glory. "And you, of course," Richard added after the fact.

It was just like her father to show up at the worst time. April hadn't seen him in years. But that was what he did. He was around for a bit, then left again. Her entire childhood was filled with him coming and going.

"Sorry, I would have called, but I didn't have your number. And the trip was kind of last minute. You know how it is."

Richard smiled at his daughter, who still stood in shock. The wind whistled through the trees, which April noticed more now that she was confronted with the silence between them.

She didn't know what to say to his excuses. They were just that, excuses. And she hated them.

"You've done a great job with the place," he said, peering out at the estate. "It looks like you've done a lot."

April shrugged, not sure what to say. She didn't want her father's approval, but at the same time, she couldn't help feeling a sense of satisfaction at his compliment.

"Thanks."

She had worked hard for this bed and breakfast. Remembering that it was opening day, she peered behind her at the customers waiting just inside the doors. Thankfully, they made themselves busy by checking out the lobby and first-floor bathrooms.

Another car began to make its way down the drive, less chaotic than her father's arrival. Her other guest for her trial opening was here, but her mind felt like it was going a hundred miles a minute.

She was going to have to try her best to make it all work. "Hey dad, could you wait for me in the lobby? Have a look around. I'm going to help these people, and then we can talk, okay?"

Though April didn't want to talk to her father, there were more important things on her mind. And she needed a reason for him to walk away so she could focus on the task at hand.

The ocean roared louder than the engine coming closer and closer. "Sure, honey," Richard replied with a smile and walked inside his old family vacation home.

First things first. The couple that came earlier needed their room and a tour of their facilities.

"What's the name?" April asked like she'd practiced a hundred times in the mirror before this day. It was obvious that this was the Miller family. It was one of two reservations, the other being a single man.

"Miller," he said confidently, smiling over at his sweetheart. "It's our first vacation in a year of marriage. Can you believe it?"

"No honeymoon?" April asked.

The woman, whose arm was wrapped tightly inside of his, replied, "No. We were too poor to go anywhere when we first got married. Now we finally get to see the beach like we wanted."

The two kissed just as the car with the other guest came to a halt outside. April felt a twinge in her stomach, maybe jealousy, maybe something else. She couldn't quite tell because her nerves of trying to make everything go right today seemed to take precedence over everything else going on inside her head.

"I'll show you to your room," April said with a smile after electronically signing them into her management software.

Just as they began up the stairs, she saw the man getting out of his car. His fully tailored suit intimidated her. She noted it for when she would check him in.

As April led the couple to their room, she couldn't help but glance back at her father in the lobby. Memories of her childhood flooded her mind. The times he'd show up unannounced and take her on adventures. The good times were always mixed with the bad. The times he'd disappear for months on end, leaving them with no explanation.

She had spent years trying to forget him and his inconsistent ways, but now he was here again, throwing her off balance.

The couple was pleased with their room, and she gave them a rundown of all the amenities. "The beach is there for you to enjoy, though it does close after dark due to the tides. And I wouldn't sit out there early in the morning either. Better to experience it midday."

They nodded, clearly taking notes in their heads for later. "On the nightstand, there's a list of great spots in town for you to visit. I recommend checking that out before you go exploring in case you find yourselves in need of food or entertainment."

It was everything April had been practicing for. She'd spent hours perfecting this exact speech. Now was her time to shine. The smile on their faces meant everything to April.

As she left their room, she noticed her father talking to the new customer in the lobby. They stared at the coffee table beside the couch. She couldn't hear what they were saying, but the man seemed to be unimpressed.

Was her father talking about the furniture, or were they talking about something completely different, like the score of the last basketball game? And did it really matter? The guest was occupied, as was her father. It seemed like a win-win to her.

April quickly made her way downstairs to welcome him and begin the check-in process. Though it didn't go as she had planned.

The man, whose name was David, looked bothered as April greeted him. He handed over his ID and credit card with a sense of reluctance, and April tried to hide her disappointment. She had been hoping for a more enthusiastic guest, someone who would be excited to be staying at her bed and breakfast. But David was different from the Millers, and he knew it.

April created this place to be something new for everyone who couldn't visit the island before. It was supposed to be an affordable, beautiful spot where people of all kinds could vacation.

David was clearly wealthy. She could tell not only by the way he held himself, but by the expensive rental in her driveway and his suitcase and sunglasses, both luxury brand.

"You reserved the King's suite, is that correct?"

His brows furrowed. "No. I reserved the Queen's suite."

Suddenly, April's cheeks felt very hot. "Of course. Right." It took her a minute to find the information on her computer. The silence between them felt stiff. "Ah, yes. Here it is."

"Finally," David said quietly and scoffed. "First I have to wait here while you give the golden guests a tour and now you can't find the right reservation."

"Sorry, sir. I'm just a little flustered today. I assure you that everything will be up to your standards."

He grumbled something under his breath. It only made April more frustrated. Her fingers couldn't hit the right keys, her hands almost shaking from the stress of the day. She felt like she couldn't do anything.

One miss-click and the entire reservation was deleted. Everything she'd been doing was erased entirely. She almost began to cry, but reminded herself that she was a strong woman, prepared to do anything for her dreams.

This was her dream.

"Um, sir. I apologize, but I do need to re-enter your information into the system. Could you tell me your address?"

The man scoffed loudly and crossed his arms in front of his chest. He looked both aggravated and defeated. "You need to reenter everything? Are you kidding me right now?"

She tried to calm him down and apologized for any inconvenience, but David's irritation only increased.

April was taken aback by his behavior. She had never encountered anyone like this before. She'd never done customer service before.

David only snatched his suitcase from his side and walked out of the house, grumbling about needing to find somewhere else to stay.

It was almost a sigh of relief to be rid of him, but April was disappointed in herself for losing one of her first clients. Her father had really thrown a wrench in her plans.

This wasn't what she pictured when she thought of her first day as a business.

Richard walked over to his daughter, who leaned against the reception desk in the entryway of her dream bed and breakfast. "What was that all about?"

April's frustration only grew as she turned to face her father. "I don't know, Dad. He was impossible. He was rude and-"

She looked at her confused father and realized that none of this was going to help either of them. "Dad, could you go into town for a little while? I just need to focus here. It's my first weekend with guests, and I can meet you there later. Sound good?"

He simply nodded and walked out of the house. From the doorway he yelled back, "And the place looks great, honey."

It was nothing like she pictured it. This was supposed to be her grand entrance into the hotel scene on the island. But instead, it was a disaster in more ways than one.

Her head fell into her hands. What was she supposed to do now? One canceled reservation, her father and her boyfriend's, if she could even call Nigel that, ex. The past two days flooded her mind.

She was drowning in the confusion and emotional whiplash she'd given herself. Three deep breaths, a hand through her hair and a sip of water later, she got back to work.

It took her a few minutes to cancel the reservation in her system. Then, she restocked the downstairs fridges and snack areas. Cleaning the lobby only took a few minutes.

April didn't want to check on the Millers yet, so she looked through her website to check for questions and reservations. A few emails came through asking about availability or the beach access, what the town had to offer.

Her responses were almost robotic by now. She knew everything about the area and had a suggestion for just about anything.

After it was all over and she could leave the property feeling okay about her guests, she walked out to her car. A wild horse ran through the field, bucking wildly.

April wished she could be as free as the mare. *Maybe someday*, she told herself as she started the car.

But right now, she had to go into town.

CHAPTER FOUR

There were several things April had on her list before she could go meet her father. One of them was taking deep breaths and walking around downtown Sandcrest.

Chuck and Barry, the town goofballs, were sitting just outside of the diner. They waved as she passed by. Though they made fun of her aspirations, they began to warm up to the idea of her bed and breakfast.

The quaint town was bustling with people, yet April found it peaceful. For the first time that day, she felt like a weight was off of her chest.

Flowers in ancient-looking pots lined the streets. Clear skies and a gentle breeze that carried a salt from the sea made fall feel alive.

The tiny sidewalk cafes had their typical clientele, the locals, plus the start of the tourists for the season.

Alice carried groceries to her car from the general store. Her arms looked heavy, but there was Lionel right behind her with several more bags. It was a perk of the small town, April realized, to have neighbors that were so willing to help out.

For a moment, she thought about running over and telling her friend all about everything that'd happened in the past twenty-four hours. But Alice quickly shuffled into her car, tossing her purse to the passenger seat.

April waved to her through the driver's side door, praying she would notice. She began to feel silly, noticing the other people walking past her, seemingly waving to no one.

It took a minute, but Alice finally looked up from the steering wheel and smiled at her. She waved back, then held up a finger.

"Call me later!" Alice yelled to her before driving off. It was something she did often, the busy woman. They would catch up at a different time. Maybe when things in April's life would calm down. Who was she kidding? It would always be this crazy.

The streets flooded with sweet music, a symphony of different songs, all folk, from the speakers of each restaurant.

She closed her eyes and took a deep breath, letting the melody wash over her. The sound of the guitar strings was soothing, and she felt her tension slipping away. Her mind was clearer now, and she felt more focused than she had all day.

Then she saw the sign for Giant's, Nigel's burger joint. It wasn't his lunch rush yet. The tables inside looked half full. April might have gotten there just in time to talk to him about the other night.

April hesitated for a moment, her hand on the door, debating whether or not she wanted to see Nigel. But curiosity got the best of her, and she found herself walking into Giant's.

She pushed the door open and was met with the smell of sizzling beef and the sound of Nigel's voice shouting orders to the kitchen staff.

The stools held several patrons, each one drinking something different. Was it too early for her to get a cocktail herself? She wanted something, anything, to ease her nerves. But in the end, April knew it wouldn't help any of the situations she'd found herself in.

Nigel's head went past the kitchen window not once, but three times. She questioned, calling over the bartender and asking for him.

She wanted to know about Lily. Had they met up since the night April walked out on dinner? Did he want her back? Was what they had just a rebound?

No. Everything was speculation. Neither of them handled that night well, but they would have to figure it out some other time. Because they were clearly preparing for something, the lunch rush probably.

April should have been preparing for something herself. And at this point, she was just putting it off. It was time to meet her father.

She left the burger joint feeling a bit defeated. She stuck her cold hands into her pockets, letting the discouragement take her. Nigel was nowhere to be found, and she had to accept that maybe he wasn't ready to talk to her yet. As she walked down the street, she tried to shake off the feeling of disappointment and focus on the task at hand.

April arrived at Millie's with ease. The popular lunch spot was a bustling cafe with bright, colorful decorations and the smell of freshly brewed coffee. As she stepped in, April took a deep breath and felt her heart flutter. She had been anticipating this moment all morning, and now it was finally here.

It was time to face her father.

Her eyes quickly scanned the room, and then she saw him - sitting in a booth with a cup of coffee warming his hands.

"Hey, kiddo," he said as she slid into the booth opposite of him. "How did the opening go?"

She shrugged. "Not my best, but I'm sure I'll get better at it."

15

The waitress took her order, remembering exactly how she liked her eggs and toast. Her father ordered the same.

"Dad, what are you doing here?"

He blinked up at her. "What do you mean? I told you, I heard about your renovations on the house. You're making it into a bed and breakfast. I wanted to see how my daughter was doing and what the place looked like now."

Normally, April would have taken that at face value. But she knew her father better than that. After all these years, she'd grown to understand that nothing ever came that easily.

"Where were you before this?"

Now she saw his eyes light up. "I was in Argentina for a while. I met the most amazing man there, who showed me how to make the most delicious empanadas. And then I went over to Chile and... and well this beautiful woman..."

As her father continued to talk, April's memory of his adventures all blended together. She barely listened to them anymore. It was good to hear what he was up to, but it was exhausting to hear about all the fun he had while he was without her.

When she was a child, she was amazed by the stories he brought back from his travels. But now it was just a reminder that he chose that life over her.

"That's great, dad," she said, sipping her coffee.

They chatted about his most recent adventures. She managed to get a few sentences in about the renovations before the food got to the table.

Her father dug into his meal with gusto, muttering his approval every few bites. April picked at her food, her mind still elsewhere. She couldn't shake the feeling that there was something her father wasn't telling her. He was here for a reason, and it wasn't just to check out the new bed and breakfast.

Richard never cared about the property before. He'd left it to rot, leaving it to April to fix up on her own. Why would he care about it now?

"So, is there something you wanted to talk to me about?" she finally asked, unable to bear the silence any longer.

His eyes bounced around the restaurant, unable to land on her face. "Uh, yes. There is something else."

Her heart pounded in her chest. It felt like time was standing still, like it was an eternity until he opened his mouth again.

"I was hoping to reconnect with you. The house is one thing. Obviously I'm interested in it. But I came to see you. To make amends."

April's heart softened a bit at the mention of making amends. She had longed for this moment for years, but now that it was here, she wasn't sure what to do.

Her eyes widened. She could hardly believe what she was hearing. Her father had never shown interest in reconciling with her before. She felt a glimmer of hope, but also a deep sense of skepticism.

Richard had a way of making her feel both angry and vulnerable at the same time, a complex combination that always left her confused. It had been that way since she was young.

"I know that I haven't been the best, but I'm here now. I want time with you," he said, his eyes full of hope.

What did this mean? What could he possibly say to make up for the time they'd lost? And yet, what right did she have to deny him the chance?

"Okay. I'm open to it," she replied quietly.

Richard's shoulders fell as he relaxed. He let out a deep breath and put a hand to his chest. "Oh, thank god. Thank you, seriously. I really appreciate that."

April nodded her head. She wanted to tell him not to mess it up, to beg her for her forgiveness. But it wasn't the time for chastising. She couldn't even think of what to say.

"The best way for us to spend time together is if we stay at the same place. What do you think? Livin' with your dad for a bit? It could be just like old times."

Old times, as in when she was an extremely young child. Otherwise, she hadn't seen enough of him to spend more than a night or two under the same roof.

His eager smile plunged right into her heart. How could she say no to that? No, really, she was trying to think of a reason.

The bed and breakfast had guests now. It was the beginning of her dreams coming true, and that came with hard work.

But then again, maybe it would be good for them to spend some time together, just the two of them. Maybe they could finally work through their issues and build a real relationship.

How could she possibly say no to family?

"Alright, sure. You can stay at the bed and breakfast in the room next to mine. How does that sound?"

Her father excitedly shuffled in his booth. He had to stop himself from clapping his hands, stopping them inches from each other. "I am so excited, honey. I can't wait for all this time together. We're going to have so much fun."

April smiled weakly, not completely convinced. She knew how easily her father's enthusiasm fizzled out. But she couldn't deny that she felt a twinge of excitement too. Maybe this was the turning point they needed.

The rest of the meal was spent in small talk, planning out their days together. Richard was brimming with ideas and stories, eager to make up for lost time. April couldn't help but feel a spark of hope that they could make this work.

As they left the restaurant, Richard slung his arm over her shoulder. "You know, I think this is going to be the start of something great."

April smiled and nodded, but inside, she wondered if it would actually become the start of something awful.

CHAPTER FIVE

Three more guests were coming the next day, which meant more preparation for April when they got back to the house.

She sent her father to make something for dinner for himself as she worked. It took him fifteen minutes of questioning before he felt confident enough to find everything he needed in the kitchen.

With a deep sigh, April started on the management system. After opening her computer, she picked out rooms for the new guests and read their requests. She would have to block off the room next to her main suite so her father could stay beside her.

There was still so much to be done to the property, including the several hundred acres of land they owned around the house.

The beautiful flowers in an ad stood out to her, but she knew there were other landscapers that would take care of the property for less. She sent emails to both, enquiring about their services.

Then she began to look for ideas for the next renovations, updating a few bathrooms and beginning to think about the ranch the property held. She still wanted to create a kind of horse ranch for all of the wild horses that roamed the property. It was supposed to be a sanctuary for them, where they would feel safe and maybe even rehabilitate. She wanted to rescue them.

How could she even think of all that while she struggled to keep the bed and breakfast running? As she closed out of all of her tabs, her heart sank. There would be time for this some other day when she didn't have to worry about doing all of this work.

April continued to prep, getting the local breakfast items on nice plates and into the fridge.

She listened to her father whistle as he worked on his meal. It was nice until she walked into the lobby and found his bags scattered across the floor.

Unease lingered in the pit of her stomach. She couldn't help but wonder if she had made a mistake in allowing her father to stay with her.

April gathered the bags and brought them to the room beside hers. It took a while to get the room ready, considering its size. It was one of the largest rooms in the house, only beaten by her owner's suite.

The bed was made with warm white sheets fresh from the dryer. She scooped up his pillows and replaced their covers with a matching set of white.

It was only by dinner time that she'd finished cleaning and making up his room. And she still had three rooms left to prepare and clean.

There would only be enough time for a quick bite to eat before getting back to the workload. April was coming to realize that this might be too much work for just one person. If she had Georgia here to help her, they would have gotten things done twice as fast.

Though of course her daughter was following her own dreams and finishing her college degree. Meanwhile, April was watching her father, taking care of him in the place she'd built. Maybe someday Georgia would help her out.

April only finished two of the three rooms before she called it quits. The other room would have to be completed before the final guest arrived.

Richard was just getting settled in for the night when April got to his room. He sat on the edge of the bed, eagerly welcoming her arrival. His bags lay discarded on the floor, and he had a soft smile on his face.

"Hey there," he said softly, patting the bed as if sizing it up. "I was just about to get ready for bed."

April nodded as she made her way towards him. She saw concern in his eyes as he looked around at his room, almost as if searching for something he had forgotten or overlooked.

"Is everything okay?" she asked, concerned.

"Uh, I was just wondering... No, it's too much to ask. Sorry," he replied, shrugging it off.

It was clear something was bothering him. "No, dad, what's up?"

"It's just the pillows... They're a little light. I was wondering if you had any that were more firm."

She had to fight the urge to roll her eyes. Instead, she plastered a smile across her face. "Of course. Let me go look."

April made her way to the linen closet, her mind racing with thoughts. As she rummaged through the shelves, she couldn't help but let out a deep sigh. All of her pillows looked the same. None were better than the others.

Would she have to do this after all of the long days she worked? The amount of work that went into running the bed and breakfast was no small feat. She hoped her father understood that.

Finally, she found a pillow that she thought might be suitable for him. She made her way back to his room, trying to put on a smile. "Here ya go, dad. How's this one?"

Richard stood in the corner of the room, next to the bathroom door. He smiled and took the pillow from her, working it in his hands. "Oh, much better."

April turned to leave the room, happy that she finally satisfied him. But then she heard a small, "Hmm."

Her feet stopped moving towards the door. She knew she had a decision to make. Did she keep walking or turn around and take care of his newest request?

Ultimately, against her better judgment, she turned to look at her father. "What's up, now, dad?" Her shoulders slumped as she waited for his response. He held a towel in his hand, massaging it with his fingers.

"It's just, these towels. Any chance you have other ones? These are kind of... scratchy."

Scratchy? Was that even a word? It definitely wasn't a word to describe her new bed and breakfast towels she'd spent so long researching. They were supposed to be top-of-the-line, some of the best brands in the business. She knew they weren't anything less than perfect.

But it was her father coming back to spend time with her. What could she say? "Of course," she replied again, this time less enthusiastically.

April made her way back to the linen closet, feeling a sense of defeat. She couldn't help but wonder if her father was intentionally making things difficult for her.

Trying to banish the thought, she shook her head,. No, that wasn't fair. He was just an old man who was used to a certain level of comfort.

She grabbed a set of her best towels. She took a deep breath, trying to shake off her frustration, and made her way back to Richard's room.

"Here you go, Dad. These are my best towels," she said, handing them over to him. It was hard not to hold her breath as he felt them.

"I guess they will have to do. Thank you, April. You're always so thoughtful," Richard replied, a smile on his face.

It took everything in her not to yell back at him. "Have a good night, dad."

He nodded and stepped into the bathroom. "Good night, sweetheart," he said before closing the door.

She was starting to feel exhausted and overwhelmed. The amount of work it took to run this place was immense, and her father's constant requests didn't make it any easier. She couldn't help but feel a little resentful.

As she changed into her pajamas, she contemplated what she would do. There had to be a way to get some help around here.

Then, it came to her. What do all businesses do when they need a helping hand? Hire someone. Someone to come in and help her with all of the tasks necessary to run the place so that she had more time to take care of the other half of a business, improving and preparing.

She should have known that she couldn't do it on her own.

As she got under the covers, April pulled her laptop onto her lap and began to type.

Attention all potential employees! Bed and Breakfast now in search of a capable, dependable front desk worker to assist in the day-to-day operations. The ideal candidate will be friendly, organized, and detail-oriented.

If this sounds like you, we would love for you to apply! We look forward to you joining the family.

She smiled as she read it back to herself. It took several minutes to finish putting the details into the posting. The pay, work schedule, and the qualifications she desired. She was almost falling asleep by the time it was completed.

With a satisfied sigh, April closed her laptop and set it on the nightstand. As she drifted off to sleep, she couldn't help but picture the new employee walking through the front door, ready to help her run the bed and breakfast.

April couldn't help but feel a sense of relief. She had taken her first step towards easing her burden.

Tomorrow would be a new day, one with hopefully less stress.

CHAPTER SIX

The next morning went by fast. April barely had time to speak with her father, though that didn't stop him from trying to claim priority over the guests checking in.

April knew she needed to focus on the day at hand. Though chaotic and anxious, she managed to make it through. For being on her own, she handled the busy morning well.

The Millers sat at a table and enjoyed their breakfast, feeding each other pastries every chance they got. She couldn't help but smile at their beautiful love.

It gave a pang in her chest, thinking about love. There was still the whole Nigel situation to debunk. Who knew what was happening there? Maybe they'd already gotten back together. April wouldn't blame him. Lily was gorgeous.

But as much as she tried to push the thought out of her head, it lingered there, gnawing at her insides. She knew she had to face her feelings eventually. Just not right then.

She had other things to deal with.

Richard waited for her at the front desk when she finished clearing out breakfast for the guests. "What's the plan for the day?" he asked.

"Well, I finally have some time. I was thinking that I would work outside. There's lots of things to do before I can start renovating the ranch. I'm going to clear out the weeds in front of the fence by the barn."

It wasn't hard to tell that Richard had no interest in cleaning up outside. He was practically wincing at the thought. "Sounds like a job for gardeners," he replied, his tone indicating that he was expecting her to agree with him.

April couldn't give in to many more of his demands, or he would run with it. "I prefer to do it myself. It's good exercise, and it'll give me a chance to get some fresh air."

"Suit yourself," he said with a shrug.

Still needing approval and wanting that olive branch she'd been promised, April continued, "Why don't you go down to the beach and relax this morning? You can get some sun and look for sea glass like you used to."

Satisfied with the suggestion, he smiled. "What a splendid idea. I'll be down there if you need anything, alright?"

There wasn't a single thing April could think of that she would need her father's help for. And that was okay with her.

Once Richard had left, April put on her work clothes and headed out to the front of the barn. She grabbed a rake and a shovel and started digging up the weeds. It was hard work, but she found it cathartic. The sun was hot on her back, and she could feel the sweat starting to trickle down her skin, but she kept at it.

The smell of farmland filled April's nose. The scent of nature was strong, and it made her smile. The leaves of the trees rustled, and she could hear the breeze as it blew through the branches. The barn's doors creaked with a low groan as it moved ever so slightly in the wind.

The other buildings around the ranch were smaller than she wanted for the horses she planned to keep there. April knew that eventually this place would need a lot of renovating to make it sustainable.

Still, she dreamed of what it could be. A place where animals would find refuge and people would find hope and love for nature.

It was a far-fetched dream, but it kept her going. April had big plans for the ranch, and she couldn't wait to start them. She wanted to build horse stables with plenty of space for the animals to roam.

She imagined the grassy open fields of her ranch, with horses running around free and wild. The sunlight glinting off their thick coats as they galloped around without a care in the world. She could almost hear them nickering and see their tails swishing in the breeze.

There would be areas for riding lessons, as well as special events such as horse therapy and summer camps for kids.

The possibilities were endless, and just thinking about it made April giddy with excitement.

It was a daunting task, but she knew that if she put all her energy into it, anything was possible.

In the middle of her daydream, April heard a sudden rustling through the trees behind the barn. She stopped, the dirty roots of a weed still lying limp in her left hand.

She wasn't afraid. It felt more like worry than fear. But worry that she was going to scare or hurt something instead of the other way around.

A long brown snout slowly pushed through the branches of the tree line less than two hundred feet away from her. The trotting mare ran into the open field.

April's heart swelled with joy at the sight of the majestic animal. She watched as the horse ran around the field, leaping and bucking with wild abandon.

Feeling breath catch in her throat, she dropped the rake and shovel, and walked slowly towards the field where the mare was. It was gorgeously brown with a wildly tangled mane and tail. Its hair shone against the sun. She didn't want to spook the mare, but she also wanted to get a closer look.

As she approached the field, she could see that the mare was running in circles, her hooves kicking up dirt and grass.

Any amount of work was worth something like this. The mare slowed down, taking time to nip at the grass. It began to walk closer to April, step by step.

She started edging slowly towards April, head down and proud, nostrils flaring. Was this the same one that she had fed so long ago? The one that was constantly searching for a new snack?

April slowly reached into the black lawn care bag at her side and pulled out a carrot. It was something she added when she thought about the time the horse left due to her lack of treats.

She had always been waiting for this moment to happen again.

She held the warm veggie in her open palm, offering it to the mare. The horse sniffed her hand, snorting softly before carefully snatching it.

April ran her hands over the silky fur on the mare's neck, feeling an overwhelming sense of peace come over her. The tall mare whinnied at her as she petted it gently. This was why she was here: to take care of beautiful beasts like this. To show people that they were worth so much more than what humans gave them.

The horse backed away slowly before beginning to trot back towards the woods. She watched from afar as the creature sprinted, kicking up dirt and grass behind her.

The horse ranch would have to start becoming more of her priority when she finally got a handle on the bed and breakfast.

Unfortunately, that didn't feel like it was happening any time soon.

April trudged back to the house, her mind still on the gorgeous mare she had just encountered. She couldn't wait to start building the horse stables and begin rescuing more animals.

There were stacks of mail waiting for her on the front desk, along with a few missed calls from potential guests. She knew she had a lot of work to do, but all she could think about was her dream for the ranch.

"Hey," her father said as he stepped into the entryway. "How was gardening?"

April shrugged, reading the several envelopes cluttering the desk. Electric company, credit card ad, even a request for a donation to a school she never attended. "It was good. But now I have all this to take care of." She held up the bills and showed him with a sarcastic smile.

"Well, the couple that was here earlier is down at the beach and they were hoping to get some towels."

Her head snapped up. "What? There weren't any towels down there or in their room?"

Richard shook his head. "Nope. I got this one from my room."

It was a wonder how he remembered to do things for himself but never other people. She wondered how her mother survived with that mindset of his. "Okay, I'll take some out there. Thank you."

April was mortified that the couple didn't have anything to dry themselves off. Maybe it was just because she hated the feeling of sand on wet feet. The way it stuck to the bottom and prickled the toes as she walked made her want to throw up ever since she was a kid.

Not just that, it was embarrassing that the bed and breakfast hadn't prepared for guests to go down to its one main attraction, the beach. She should have been more prepared than this.

She looked up and saw her dad still staring at her. She stood to leave. When her father didn't leave the desk, April's chest slowly sank with dread. "What?"

He bit his lip. "I was just wondering if maybe you could get me some Tylenol? I'm having a dreadful headache."

April's head was about to start throbbing if her father didn't stop making demands. Of course, she would have to get him something to help with his headache. He would never pack something like that for himself, even though April and her mother would never leave the house without it.

Just as she opened her mouth to answer him, she saw the Millers coming up the stairs from the beach soaking wet. She stumbled on her words, thinking about how quickly she would have to run to grab them towels before they got to the entryway.

"Here," she said, throwing her dad her purse from behind the counter. "It's in a white bottle in there. Take what you need."

Sprinting through the lobby, she grabbed two towels from the linen closet and made her way outside. She was hoping that they would be up to their standard, since they weren't up to her father's.

As April approached the beach, she could see that the Millers had already made it to the entryway, dripping wet. She quickly handed them the towels and apologized for the inconvenience.

"Thank you so much," the wife said, taking a towel and rubbing it over her arms. "We didn't realize how cold the water was until we got in."

April gave them both a sympathetic smile. "No problem at all. Sorry for not having them down at the beach."

As the couple began their trek back down to the water, April's phone vibrated in her pocket. It was hard to resist the urge to yell. What could it be now? What else could she have to deal with today?

She hoped the email logo wasn't another room request or complaint. Opening it immediately, she read the subject line.

Applicant to Attention all potential employees!

April almost teared up at the relief. It took seconds to pull up the application and read through the glowing resume with recommendations and hospitality experience.

She dialed the number right away and tapped her foot impatiently as she listened to the ring. Three rings in and she had almost given up hope, until she heard a woman's voice.

"Hello, is this Millie?"

"Yes, it is! Is this about the bed and breakfast?"

"Yes," April responded reluctantly. She wished she would have waited a few more minutes before responding to the application. But she needed help as soon as possible.

A few seconds of silence made her shoulders tense. Would this scare away her only applicant so far?

"Great! You guys are fast. I just applied not too long ago."

Relief flooded her. "When can you come in for an interview?"

"Today, if you'd like! I don't have anything going on."

April almost wanted to jump into the air with excitement. She had been so worried about finding help for the bnb, but now that her dream was coming true, she couldn't contain herself.

She ran through the list of chores she had to complete for the day and found that she could manage to fit in an interview if Millie didn't need too much time.

"Absolutely! Whenever you can make it would be great."

"I can be there in about two hours?"

The excitement was almost overwhelming. "That sounds perfect!" April said, trying hard not to sound too eager. She thanked Millie for her interest and provided directions to the estate before they hung up.

Everything was falling into place. April would hire this woman to help out around the place, and she would be able to start on the ranch. It was all coming together.

Though, she was getting ahead of herself. Millie would have to prove that she could handle the work that April couldn't manage on her own.

But after that, April would be free.

CHAPTER SEVEN

When Millie arrived, April welcomed her with open arms and ushered her into the lobby area.

A beaming smile showed Millie's white teeth, and her eyes were sparkling with excitement. Her blonde hair was pulled up in a ponytail, and she wore a mid-length blue dress that hugged her well.

Millie was taller than April expected. Though she wore heels, April knew that Millie would still be hovering over her without them. She was lanky and thin, legs that went on forever and arms that hung low at her sides.

It wasn't what April expected, but she liked something about her. And she wanted more than anything a competent person to help her around the estate.

She wanted to give her a tour and explain all the responsibilities that came with the job. After introductions, they did just that.

April gestured grandly as they walked through what used to be the living room. "This area is meant to be a place where guests can relax and enjoy each other's company. You would be responsible for keeping this space tidy and inviting."

"It's lovely," Millie said, eyeing the simplistic and modern furniture Georgia and April had spent hours picking out. It was always nice to receive compliments on the style.

April smiled proudly, grateful for the hard work she had put into decorating the space. "Thank you! We try to make it feel like a home away from home for our guests. And of course, the cleanliness is a top priority."

She led Millie through the rest of the house, showing her the bedrooms and the dining area. "You'll be in charge of preparing the small breakfast items and keeping the kitchen clean," April explained. "And you'll also be responsible for cleaning the guest rooms and ensuring that everything is well-stocked."

Millie nodded eagerly. "It sounds like a lot of work, but I think I can handle it."

"Were you in charge of all of this at your last job in hospitality? I saw you worked for a hotel not too long ago."

April looked at her as they made their way back to the welcome desk. "I'm used to the cleaning and prep work. I'll just have to learn the computer system. That's different everywhere you go." Her smile made April feel good.

What was it that Millie exuded that caught April's attention? She was just so captivating, April couldn't get herself to look away. Maybe it was confidence or a kind of charm.

"Well, you'll have plenty of time to become familiar with the system," April said. "Why don't we go over some of your resume qualifications? That way I can get a better feel for if you would be a good fit here."

Millie nodded, and they sat down behind the desk in the lobby. April opened up Millie's file and scanned through it, pointing out some of her experience in hospitality and customer service as well as her past roles in team management.

April was impressed. She could see that Millie was an experienced worker.

"And what would you do if you encountered a disgruntled guest?"

Millie leaned forward, her expression serious. "Well, I would listen to their concerns and try to understand their perspective. Then, I would apologize on behalf of the establishment and offer them a solution that would rectify the situation to the best of my abilities. It's important to make sure our guests feel heard and valued."

April nodded, satisfied with Millie's response. "Great answer. And what about managing multiple tasks at once? This job can get pretty hectic sometimes."

"I'm used to managing a busy lobby," she replied confidently. "In fact, I find that I work best under pressure."

"That's impressive," April said, trying to hide the excitement in her voice. "I love that. Could you tell me about a time when you were forced to work in a chaotic environment?"

Millie put a finger to her chin in thought, but April wondered if it was just a charade. She had to have all of her answers memorized by how well they sounded. "There was this one time," she finally began, "I was working at the customer service desk of a department store and the customers were getting quite rowdy."

April had never had to work somewhere like that, so she didn't understand the work that happened behind the counter.

"My manager was on break, so I had to take charge. I called up my other employees and organized the customers into neat lines. It worked really well, actually. They all listened up after that," she explained with a smile.

It was hard to find flaws in Millie. But April liked that she'd managed to find the best in town. It felt good to know that such a good worker was interested in helping her out.

"And do you have any references?"

She nodded her head and pulled out a piece of paper with handwritten names and numbers. "Sorry, it's not more professional. I wanted their permission before you called them. So I had to get their okay last minute."

Looking through the names, there wasn't one she didn't recognize. Several were from big name hotels and the other two were local business owners.

"Okay, and-"

April was quickly interrupted by a man who checked in earlier that day. His bald head reflecting the sun behind him. "Sorry to bother you," he said, his voice so soft they both had to lean forward to hear him. "But I was wondering if you knew any local places to get lunch."

Before she could open her mouth to tell the man that she would help, Millie stood. With a smile, she grabbed one of the lists of local spots from behind the desk and handed it to the man.

Impressed, April raised her brows. But then she did something that sealed her a position at the bed and breakfast.

"If you look here, you'll find the best places in town. I recommend these two," she said, pointing to the paper. "You're going to take this road and then..."

Millie droned on, explaining how to get to each of the diners in town before coming back to her seat and sending the man off. With a smile, he got into his car and drove off towards town.

It was no question that she wouldn't call and check on Millie's performance. She showed exactly what she was capable of in just a few minutes. It was impressive how eloquently she handled the situation.

If April experienced this level of customer service somewhere, she would have a hard time ever leaving. And that's exactly the kind of help she needed.

"You're hired," she said without a second thought.

"Seriously?"

April nodded, a smile spreading across her face. Who wouldn't hire someone as perfect as her?

31

Millie beamed with joy, her eyes sparkling. "Thank you so much! I won't let you down."

"I have no doubt about that," April said, returning Millie's smile. "When are you available to start?"

Still flabbergasted, Millie stumbled on her words. "Uh, immediately."

It felt like a weight had been lifted off of April's shoulders. She sighed in relief. She finally had someone to help her with the bed and breakfast.

April felt grateful that she had found such a competent and charming addition to her staff. She knew that with Millie's help, the bed and breakfast could thrive beyond her wildest dreams.

"Fantastic. Let's get you started on the computer system. We have a guests arriving in a few hours and I want to make sure everything is perfect."

Millie eagerly agreed and filled out her employment paperwork as April set up the system and wrote out instructions. It only took a few minutes to get her system ready. All Millie would have to do was press a few buttons and then show the guest to their room.

Just as April was about to finish explaining everything to Millie, her phone buzzed in her pocket. She took it out and saw that she had a text from Nigel.

She slipped her phone back into her pocket and waited until Millie felt comfortable with the program. Then, she stepped away and checked her phone.

Any chance you could come over and talk tonight?

It was the moment she'd been dreading. She didn't want to talk about Lily. But she knew they had to. Whatever was between April and Nigel, it felt different now.

Maybe it was her pushing back, running away from the first sign of insecurity. But she couldn't help it. She didn't like how his ex-girlfriend showed up out of the blue.

It didn't help that Nigel didn't say the right things when he had the chance. She told him to figure out how he felt. Maybe he finally had.

CHAPTER EIGHT

The night air was cool on her skin as she walked down the street. Even in the dark, she could see that there were still people out and about, enjoying their time. She was slightly envious.

Though she agreed to have dinner at Nigel's house, she worried about how it would go. In her heart, she still hadn't forgiven him for how he acted that night Lily came into town.

And it was her first night away from the bed and breakfast since the soft launch. He had to have known how big of a deal it was. She hoped he felt special to know that she would do that for him.

In fact, if she hadn't found Millie, she wouldn't have agreed to meet him. There would have been too many available excuses.

I have to get the room ready for the guests. It's too busy tonight. Maybe another time?

She imagined writing out those texts instead of the unenthusiastic acceptance she ended up sending.

The street was dark, the only light coming from streetlights that hadn't been dimmed into the night. The night air brushed her skin, sending chills down her spine. Thankfully, she'd remembered to bring her sweater.

A hint of pine trees and a cool breeze that smelled slightly of the ocean blew past her face. The only sound filling her ears, the soft crunch under her feet.

Downtown was different than it was during the day. The bustling center of town was now quiet and peaceful. She wished knocking on his door gave her the same peace. Instead, it made her heart pound and her mouth dry.

April eagerly waited to see his face appear in the doorway. But when it finally did, her nerves took over. Her body wanted to run, but she kept her feet firmly planted.

"Hi," he said, his eyes taking her in with a warmth she hadn't expected.

"Hi," she replied, her voice barely above a whisper.

Nigel smiled, and a hint of relief came over his face. He opened the door wider and stepped aside so that April could enter. "Come in," he said.

She walked into the same place she'd been that night, looking around for clues that Lily had been over. Jealousy seemed to take over.

But how could she blame him? She was a gorgeous woman who clearly came back into town to see him. And April was just someone he'd met not that long ago. They'd only known each other for a few months, unlike the history she assumed lay between Nigel and Lily.

April sat on the couch and waited for him to speak. A few times he opened his mouth to speak and no words came out. She waited patiently for the words she wanted to hear.

"I'm really sorry about what happened. I wasn't expecting that at all. I know I handled it poorly. It was just a big misunderstanding."

That was close to the speech April had in her head. "I appreciate that. And I accept your apology."

"Thank you," Nigel said, his hands clasped together like in prayer. "I can't tell you how much that means to me."

She slowly started to remember why she fell in love with him in the first place.

His intellect and wit was something she admired, because it reminded her of her own. She could always talk to him about anything without feeling judged or embarrassed.

He was always so sure of himself and yet gentle when it came to her. His eyes were intense and captivating, drawing her in like a moth to flame.

Nigel sat beside her, leaving enough room between them for an extra person. She could tell he was being cautious of her feelings, and she appreciated that.

"So how did the soft opening go? The first guests should be in now, right?"

April relaxed a little at the change of topic. "It was good. I was a little nervous at first, but everything ended up okay. The couple who checked in seemed really nice. But I did lose one of my first guests."

"Lose?"

Her mouth just continued to move, spewing out all of the facts of the last two days.

April's expression darkened. "He had some high expectations and I made a few mistakes. He had no patience. It wasn't a good fit, but I learned from it."

Nigel nodded understandingly. "It happens. You're doing something new, and there's bound to be a learning curve. I'm sure things will get better with time."

"Right, well..."

April considered telling him the truth about her father showing up and distracting her from the opening. In the end, she couldn't hold it in. The stress was building up, and hiring an extra hand could only help so much. She needed to let loose.

A hand nervously went to her mouth as she explained it all. "My dad showed up. I haven't seen him for quite some time. He's kind of come and gone in my life. And he just happened to come right as the man was coming. So I mean, technically I was distracted. I probably would have handled it better if he wasn't there."

"Oh? What was that like? What did your father want?"

April went on to tell him everything Richard said. She left out the part about wanting to call Nigel a few times so that she could tell him all of this sooner. She just wanted to give him the space he needed.

The space to figure out if he wanted to get with his ex-girlfriend. Who she realized they hadn't spoken about yet. What did she want? Did they meet up?

Aside from the short apology, she realized she was the one who had been talking. But Nigel had the answers to the real questions between them.

"I'm sorry. Here I am droning on and on about me. What about you? What happened the past few days with... Lily?"

Nigel took a deep breath. His shoulders relaxed as if he was relieved to finally be able to tell her the truth.

"Well, she did try to see me again, this time at work. She came to Giant's for lunch one day."

That gave April a bad feeling in the pit of her stomach. She crossed her arms in front of her chest, suddenly feeling like she was taking up so much space in the room.

"She came to see you at work? What did she want?" April asked, her voice laced with suspicion.

Nigel's expression turned pensive. "She told me that she's here for work. That's why she came back into town."

Though it should have brought her relief, she didn't feel relaxed at all. Far from it, in fact. Because she knew that Lily could always have other intentions. Once she didn't tell the man she was trying to get back about.

When she didn't respond, Nigel continued, "She's supposed to be here for a week. But then she told me that she might be moving back here after that."

April gulped, feeling her throat dry up as she attempted to swallow hard. "What does she do for work?"

"I'm not sure, to be honest. She didn't tell me. I asked her to leave after that."

The only good thing in the entire story was that Nigel didn't want to talk to her. Otherwise, each detail made April more nervous. Was there a chance they would get back together? She didn't want to be the fool who fell for someone that was in love with someone else the entire time.

She'd seen those movies. They didn't end up well for people like her.

"What happened between the two of you?"

The question was out there now, and Nigel paused. She looked at him, reading the emotions that played across his face. He seemed nervous, as if he had something to hide.

"We were engaged," Nigel said finally, looking away from her gaze. "But it didn't last long."

April could hardly believe her ears. Her jaw dropped in shock as she tried to find the right words to respond.

April felt like she had been slapped in the face. Engaged? She hadn't expected that at all. It was like everything in her world suddenly shifted and changed, even though nothing had actually happened yet.

Everything felt different, as if a veil of uncertainty and doubt had descended upon them, clouding their relationship with it's thickness.

For a moment, April was speechless. She didn't know what to say or how to respond to such an unexpected turn of events. She knew Nigel had dated Lily before but engaged? Something told her there was much more to the story than he was letting on, and that thought made her feel uneasy.

"Engaged? You were engaged? To Lily?" she asked, her voice barely above a whisper.

"Yes. But it was so short-lived. We were in love once. She broke things off a month later."

April could feel her heart rate picking up speed as she tried to process what she had just heard. Her stomach lurched, making her nauseous.

Engaged? It was a lot to take in, and she wasn't sure how she felt about it.

There was a sharp pang of jealousy that hit her, but she tried to push it aside. She didn't want to be that kind of person. But she couldn't shake off the feeling that something wasn't right.

April couldn't help but feel a sense of betrayal wash over her. She had fallen for a man who was still hung up on his ex-fiancée. It was like she was just a placeholder until Lily came back into the picture. Her heart felt heavy with disappointment and despair.

Not only were they engaged, but she was the one to break things off. She didn't want to jump to conclusions. But it was hard not to hear all of this news at once.

April wanted to storm out of the apartment again, but this time never come back. But she looked at the man beside her. His eyes full of regret and confusion.

Whatever the ending, she needed to try and stick it out. It was worth it for her to stay. At least until she knew more.

"Maybe we should just eat dinner," she suggested, and stood to move to the table.

Nigel kept his distance, but followed her to his own seat. The dinner was nothing less than uncomfortable. They ate in almost pure silence. Both unsure of what to say to make things better.

April wanted this man more every day, but today it was hard to see their future together. She had so many more questions.

It felt like it'd been an eternity when she finally left the apartment. She'd given Nigel a hug, that felt like nothing was wrong between them. But as she walked to her car down the chilly street, she kept telling herself that something had changed.

Their relationship wasn't what it was just a few days ago. She wanted so desperately to go back there. To be happy with him again. Maybe someday soon, after she processed all of this, they could go back to normal.

Whatever normal was.

CHAPTER NINE

Before Millie could come in the next morning, April had a laundry list of things to do. But she didn't care because when her new hire arrived, the weight would be lifted from her shoulders.

She could handle the rush in the meantime. It was a welcome distraction from Lily and Nigel.

All she could see was a ring on Lily's finger, delicately placed there by Nigel. It wasn't that he was engaged before. She had been married not too long ago herself, for a long time.

It was the fact that his ex-fiance was back at his doorstep, practically begging to get back together with him. And she had no idea that he was once engaged.

They hadn't been given a chance to talk about their past relationships, but at least April told him upfront about her ex-husband.

April had been in love before, and failed miserably at it. She wanted to love again, and make sure that this time it was for good. But now she was left with doubts that maybe it wasn't meant to be.

Love was hard. Was she ready for something hard? Like facing what happened between Nigel and his ex and how he handled the situation with her?

It felt like he kept Lily a secret. As if she was something he needed to hide. The only reason he told her about them was because she happened to be there when Lily showed up that night.

Would he have said anything if she wasn't there? Maybe.

Maybe not.

The thought made her heart ache, and she tried her best to push it aside. She had a business to run, after all.

As she cleaned up after breakfast, she saw her father step into the lobby. *Here we go again*, she thought.

"I can't get my tv to work in there. Any chance you could take a look at it today while I'm out?"

The request was simple enough. Even easier now that she had Millie to look after the other guests. "Sure. What are you doing today?"

"Well, I was thinking about going shopping in town. Get some new towels and maybe some pillows."

38

It took everything in April not to roll her eyes. Of course, he was going to replace the things he hated about the place so far. "Sounds good," she replied in a straightforward tone with a frown across her face.

Behind them, Millie walked into the lobby, her hands full. In one hand she held a warm coffee, in the other a bag full of her belongings for the day. She sat behind the desk and spread out what she needed.

It was nice to have a self-starter for an employee. "Good morning," Millie said, bright-eyed and cheery. "Have the Millers checked out of their room yet?"

"I don't believe so. They should be down any minute."

Millie leaned across the desk with a smile. "Would you like me to go check on them?"

April watched her father walk away, presumably to get ready to go out. The lobby began to fill with guests as they began their days. "No, that's alright. I think they'll be coming down soon," she said.

Millie shrugged. "Alright. Well, I'll go set up for the guest checking in today."

"And I'll clean the Millers room when they're done, so you don't have to worry about that reset with the new guests."

April couldn't help but smile. It felt so nice to have someone else helping her for a change. For the first time in a long time, she felt a glimmer of hope that maybe she would get time to start on other renovations soon.

They worked together so well, April just knew Millie was going to fit in at the house. It was like they were two gears in the same clock, both working towards one goal, but each with their own part.

April wondered if it would always be like this. When would her new worker show her flaws? Because so far, she was nothing short of excellent.

The two went their separate ways, Millie checking on the rooms for new guests and April checking on the Millers.

Just before April reached the door, it opened, almost hitting her in the head. "Woah!" she yelled out.

"Oh my gosh. So sorry," the wife cried out from the other side of the door. "We were just leaving. I had no idea anyone was out here!"

"It's alright," April replied, rubbing her forehead and letting out the held breath from the fear. "Do you need help with your bags?"

She peered around the door to find the couple shuffling their luggage out. "No, I think we've got it from here," the man replied. He looked at his wife, who raised her brows at him. "Well, I've got it from here."

His wife smiled, which almost made April chuckle. They were such a cute couple, it was hard not to be happy around them. April pushed down the memories of Nigel, pretending like her own love life wasn't a mess.

"We appreciate you staying with us. I hope you enjoyed it!"

The wife stepped to the side and let her husband fumble with the bags down the stairs. "This was the best trip we've had. Though... we haven't gone on many. Still! It was so wonderful. We wouldn't have changed a single thing about it."

April's heart melted at the couple's sweet story. She wanted to hear more, so she followed them outside, taking a few moments to talk with the couple about their trip and their experience at the hotel.

"It was just wonderful," the man said, his eyes twinkling with excitement.

"The views were breathtaking! It was like nothing I've ever seen before." He stopped on the stairs and hugged his wife close, turning back towards April. "We will definitely be telling everyone about this place."

April couldn't help but feel a sense of pride at the compliment. It was guests like these that would make it all worth it. "Thank you, that means a lot to me," she replied, her eyes glowing with happiness.

She watched as their car pulled away, the happy couple kissing in the back seat. As she went back up to their room, she hoped she would see them again soon.

An antique four-poster bed stood in the center of the room. A floral comforter covered it, with a matching throw at the end of the bed. The lavender room spray made the space feel like a garden. A thick down comforter and extra pillows gave the bed a decadent feel.

It was one of April's favorite rooms in the house so far. The dresser held several local collectibles from the shops downtown. It was made of dark, almost black wood, worn smooth over time by a thousand hands touching its surface.

April let her fingers glide across its top, taking in each of the beautiful pieces she'd hand-picked to sit there. The rustic clock, the hand painted vase and the...

Something was missing from the top of the dresser. It only would have been more obvious if there was a dust etching of the object on top of the wood. Though she wanted her guests to feel free to move things, there wasn't really a reason to move around an antique jewelry box.

No one would confuse that for a freebie at a hotel like soaps and robes.

April carefully searched the room as she cleaned. She stripped the bed, collected everything from the bathroom, and went through every drawer in the dresser and the two nightstands. No corner or drawer was left unturned.

They were so kind to her. There's no chance that they could have stolen her items from the room, right? Her perfectly curated room felt a little more empty, like something was missing. It was a hole that her knick-knack had left behind.

April's mind raced as she tried to piece together what could have happened to the jewelry box. It was hard to jump to the conclusion that the Millers stole it. She couldn't help but feel a sense of violation that someone would steal from her, especially after they had such a wonderful stay.

She took a deep breath and reminded herself that she had to handle this professionally. She couldn't let this ruin her guests' experience or her reputation.

April quickly headed to the front desk, where Millie was already on the phone with a guest. She waved at April to let her know she'd be with her in a moment.

When she hung up the phone a moment later, she said, "Are you okay with the new guest coming in an hour before check-in? The room is already ready. I told them that I would call them back."

"Sure, sure," April said, waving it away. She had more serious matters to attend to. "I just cleaned the Millers room and something is missing. Can you believe that?"

Millie's brows furrowed. "What? What's missing?"

April was glad that it wasn't just her thinking that the couple didn't seem the type to steal. It felt out of place not just for her. "This little jewelry box we thrifted. It was so cute. It fit the room perfectly and now it's just gone."

"Oh my gosh. That's so strange that they would take something like that. Are you sure you checked everywhere? Maybe it just fell behind something."

She thought back to the room and how thoroughly she checked as she cleaned every nook and cranny. "I'm almost positive that it's not in that room anymore."

"That sucks," Millie said, a hand on her chin in thought.

"What do I do now? Am I supposed to report it stolen or something?"

She really didn't have a protocol for this. It was her first week having real guests stay at the bed and breakfast. There weren't any rules in the manual. They would have to figure this out on their own.

"No!" Millie cried out. "You can't report them. What if they didn't take it, or it was just an accident? They'll give you the worst review ever. I've seen it before."

April would do anything to avoid a bad review. It could take down businesses. Especially small ones like hers.

She'd seen it firsthand as a new lawyer. Some people wrote bad reviews, and it ruined young law students who were looking for a way into the industry.

Sure, bed and breakfasts were different. April thought they probably hinged more on reviews due to their hand in the service industry. Which meant she had to be even more careful.

"I don't have any reviews yet. That would ruin me. You really think they would do that?"

She shrugged in response. Millie's expression softened with understanding. "I'll make a note of it in the system, and we'll keep an eye out for it. Hopefully, it's just a misunderstanding and it will turn up soon."

"What would I do without you," April said with a smile.

Still, it annoyed April that something mysteriously went missing. She couldn't shake the feeling of unease that settled in the pit of her stomach. What if it wasn't just a simple misunderstanding? What if it was stolen?

She finished up her tasks for the morning, but found herself stealing glances at the room with the missing jewelry box every so often. It was a reminder of all the unanswered questions.

She wanted to believe that it was just a mistake but deep down she knew better.

CHAPTER TEN

With the addition of Millie, the bed and breakfast was running low on funds. It was just breaking even with the amount of current reservations and the renovation budget she set aside to continue her endeavors.

Who knew when she would be able to replenish the reno budget? April decided she needed to save as much as possible. Which meant doing any renovations and repairs herself.

She grabbed a few supplies from the hardware store and returned to the bed and breakfast. She started with the bathroom in the corner, the one that still needed to be finished. The first step was new tile flooring, and she was determined to do it herself.

April laid out all her materials in the bathroom, carefully planning what she would use and for what. She began chipping away at the old tile with a hammer and chisel.

As she worked, she hummed along to herself, lost in her own little world of creation.

"Hey, honey?" her father said as he stepped into the bathroom doorway.

A sweaty April stood straighter. "What's up dad?"

"Are you getting rid of the floors in here? I liked that pattern."

Of course he did. And he was going to voice his opinion on the new, plainer pattern she picked out. "Well, I'm putting this new one in."

"Want some help?" he asked with a hopeful smile.

April considered his offer. It would be nice to have an extra hand at cracking open the floor. The work itself was more physically difficult than she anticipated. Her forearms ached.

Not to mention, he wanted to reconnect with her. This could be one of those great father/daughter moments they'd been waiting for. She wanted to give him a chance. Now she needed to put the time in, just like he was offering to do.

"Sure, grab a sledgehammer."

He grabbed a hammer from the pile of tools and put on safety goggles and gloves as she continued to swing at the floor. He put a hand on her shoulder to get her attention. "You know if you hold it with your hands further apart, it'll be easier."

She nodded her head and tried the new positioning. They both swung at different parts of the floor, getting extra careful when they were getting close to the last bits.

With one final blow, the last tile cracked, and the old floor was finally gone. The broken pieces lay across the floor until April was able to sweep them all up into a bin. They both stepped back to admire their handiwork, panting heavily.

"Well, that was fun," her father said, removing his goggles.

April smiled. "Yeah, it was. Thanks for the help, dad."

She felt a twinge of guilt. She had been so caught up in her own world of the bed and breakfast. Maybe it was time to focus on reconnecting.

"Do you want help with the new tile?" he asked as he grabbed it from the box.

She winced as he pulled out the modern white and gray patterned tile. It was the exact opposite of his style, but fit the room well.

"This one, really? I've seen it in every new property this year. You want this to be the one?"

April rolled her eyes, trying to hide her annoyance. She understood her father's taste was more traditional, but she was going for a modern look.

"Yes, this one. It'll look great, trust me."

Her father shrugged. "Alright, if you say so."

They worked in silence, carefully laying out the new tile. April made sure every piece was perfectly lined up on her end of the bathroom. Her father worked on the pieces by the door while she worked on the parts by the shower.

"Make sure you measure everything out. Don't want the pattern to be uneven when we're done," Richard said as he pasted the floor and stuck down another gray tile.

She tried not to sigh loudly. "Right. I got it, dad."

As they got to the end of their first rows of tile, April's heart fell into her stomach. The last tile sat in her hand. She stared at it, then back at the floor, then back at it.

The tile wasn't going to fit in with the pattern. If she cut it, it would fit between her second to last tile and the wall, but the pattern for the rest of the room would be off. They would be missing portions of the lines when they didn't need to.

Something was wrong here. She bit her lip and looked over at her father, sheepishly. "Uh, dad. I think I messed it up." Frustrated, she threw down her trowel.

Her father picked up the tile, eyeing it carefully. He looked back at her, his brow furrowed in concentration. She felt a flush of embarrassment creep up her neck; she had been so careful with this project, and now she was going to have to redo an entire row.

"Looks like you made a mistake when you measured. And you're putting too little of the mortar on. It's not going to stick well," her dad said, pointing to exactly the places where she went wrong.

She groaned in frustration and felt her cheeks flush. Considering the warning she'd just received, she should have been more careful.

"Let me talk you through it," her father said, and he proceeded to give her tips on how to properly measure the tiles so they would fit in the room evenly, as well as how best to lay them down with the right amount of mortar.

April begrudgingly listened, grateful for his advice but feeling frustrated that he always seemed to want things his way. Even though she made a mistake, she didn't need a speech to get things right this time.

It was hard enough doing the project, but to have to listen to mister perfect need everything his way, it was exhausting.

She knew she made a mistake. Of course, her father was just trying to correct it. But everything she did around him was a mistake. He needed more, needed something newer, better.

He never complimented, only corrected.

April looked behind her at the row her father did. Every tile lined up perfectly, nothing out of place, and each piece fit snugly against its neighbor. He had managed to get it right on the first try, something she couldn't say for herself.

And yet, hers wasn't that far off of his. The amount of mortar under the tiles was the same. The only thing different was the slight measurement she missed.

Still, she listened through his speech on how to lay out the cold muck to stick the tiles to the floor just as he did. April didn't know if it was the 'right' way, but it was Richard's way.

As they continued to work, April couldn't help but feel angry. She was tired of always being the one who had to listen and follow instructions. She had her own ideas and opinions, but it seemed like her father never wanted to hear them.

She had always wanted to prove herself to him, to show him that she was capable of doing things her way. But every time she tried, he was quick to point out her mistakes and correct her.

She wondered if he even realized how much his constant criticism was affecting her. Did he know that every time he corrected her, she felt like a failure?

April tried to push those thoughts aside and focused on the task at hand. She carefully measured each tile, making sure to get it just right. And when it came time to lay them down, she finally got the row back on track.

Her father nodded in approval, but April felt no satisfaction. Instead, her anger simmered just below the surface. She couldn't take it anymore - the constant criticism, the lack of acknowledgment for her hard work and effort.

For now, she would have to grin and bear it. In just a few weeks, he would probably be gone again.

CHAPTER ELEVEN

Deciding to take her mind off the stress she'd been under, April decided to take a more relaxed approach the next morning. She took a stroll around the quaint downtown area. The sun was just coming up, painting the sky in shades of pink and purple. A light breeze rustled through the trees, providing welcome relief from the summer heat of season past.

The city felt like it was coming to life. Again, she felt at home in its streets.

The sound of creaking doors and laughing children reached her ears. The murmur of conversation and the clatter of dishes.

April passed a coffee shop, and the delicious aroma of coffee wafted out. She was tempted to stop at the small café for a latte.

For a split second, she thought about the time she and Nigel went to the same coffee spot. She didn't want to think about Nigel, but she couldn't stop herself from wondering what else he might be up to.

She cared for him more than she wanted to admit.

Maybe she should text him. That way, she'd know what he was up to and if he was thinking about her too.

No, she thought, shaking her head. She should call. It was the right thing to do. Plus, he was one of the only people that could help her relax after a day like she was having.

The phone rang and rang as she listened intently. April sighed as she heard the phone ring for the fourth time. Still, no answer. She couldn't help but feel disappointed, although in hindsight it was foolish to hope that Nigel would pick up her call without any warning.

The sound of Nigel's voice on the other end of the call excited her, but she quickly realized it was the same voicemail recording she'd heard several times before.

April continued to walk downtown, but she knew exactly where she had to go. Giant's, Nigel's burger joint. There, she could talk to him face to face.

As April approached Giant's, the familiar smell of sizzling beef patties and freshly cut fries greeted her. She pushed open the door, the sound of the bell announcing her arrival.

Several patrons sat at the bar, while almost all of the booths were full. The sound of the bustling crowd made it difficult to hear anyone more than five feet away.

She searched the bar for Nigel, not finding him anywhere. She could pick him out of a crowd like it was nothing. But it was busier than normal for this time of day. He was probably in the back helping the cooks like he always did.

April walked towards the kitchen, the sounds of the sizzling grill and the clanging of pots and pans getting louder as she approached. She could hear Nigel's booming voice over the noise, barking out orders to the cooks.

As she looked through the kitchen window from a stool at the bar, she expected to see him walk by. But after a minute or so, he didn't. They must have really been swamped for him to not even make an appearance bustling about the place like usual.

Searching for the bartender she knew, April looked left and right. When she finally found his face, she was surprised to see it leaning across the bar, talking to a beautiful woman.

He wasn't usually that friendly with newcomers. She struggled to see a face to get some clarity on the situation. And that's when her stomach dropped.

Sitting across from the bartender, folded over in laughter, was Lily. It was Nigel's ex-girlfriend. She was at his restaurant again.

April couldn't believe it. She felt a pang of jealousy in her chest that she couldn't ignore. It was clear now that she still had feelings for Nigel. This would be the third time she'd tried to talk to him this week.

Nigel said that he didn't talk to her, but maybe that wasn't true. Maybe her intuition was right, that they were talking again. That she was trying to steal away Nigel and run off into the sunset.

April's mind was in a frenzy as she watched the pair from afar, unable to tear her gaze away. The woman's laughter was like a knife to her gut, twisting and turning until it felt like she would never be able to breathe properly again.

It wasn't like she was talking to Nigel. But the fact that she would show up at his place of work so many times, it infuriated April.

She fantasized about how she would march up to Lily, give her a piece of her mind, and let her know that she was not going to stand for this little plan she had concocted.

April imagined herself telling Lily that she knew exactly what she was trying to do and that it wasn't going to work. She pictured the look on Lily's face as the words came out of her mouth.

The surge of power at the thought surprised her, knowing that if it ever did come down to it, she could stand up for herself and win any argument. She was still a lawyer at heart, after all.

April wanted to ask her what she was thinking, coming here so often. But she knew the consequences of such an outburst would be more harmful than beneficial.

Walking out of the restaurant, both enraged and disappointed, April continued down the street, hoping that it would soon help her relax.

***

"And that's how my last date ended in disaster," Alice explained.

Beth shrugged her shoulders. "They all end in disaster one way or another. Just be glad it ended on the first date."

Kellie laughed, then sipped from her wine glass. "Could you imagine what would've happened if you found out he was a jerk on the fourth date? You would've spent way too much time with him."

Surrounded by her new friends, April felt comfortable for the first time in days. The meeting of the group of women who came to Sandcrest looking for new lives happened every Monday night. And April was always excited to go.

The other women's stories made her feel better about her morning of finding Lily at Giant's. They all had trouble in the love life department. Well, except for Kellie, who happened to find her soul mate visiting town a few months ago.

They were all jealous, even if they didn't say it.

April smiled, feeling grateful for the camaraderie that came with spending time with other women who understood her struggles. She felt relieved that she could speak openly without fear of being judged.

As the conversation continued, April couldn't help but think about Nigel. She had been so distracted by Lily's appearance that she had almost forgotten why she had gone to Giant's in the first place.

She wondered if he was still there, talking to Lily. The thought made her blood boil again. How could he not see through her manipulations?

But then again, maybe she was just being paranoid. Maybe Nigel really wasn't talking to Lily, and it was all in her head.

"And what about you, April?" Alice said, her smile inviting and warm.

She took a deep breath, preparing herself and her words carefully. But it didn't matter how put together she wanted to look. Her words came out like lava spewing from the top of a mountain.

"Nigel's ex-girlfriend is in town. I don't know how to feel about it. Obviously, we just started dating not that long ago. We're still figuring things out. But I was at his house when she came by and asked to talk to him. It was so uncomfortable."

Beth gasped, clutching her chest with her hand. "What? She came to his place while you were over there? What gives her the confidence?"

"Well, she's gorgeous for one," April said, resentment on her lips.

Kellie shook her head. "That doesn't give her the right to just waltz into his life like that. I mean, what's her endgame?"

"I don't know," April said, feeling defeated. "But she keeps showing up at his restaurant. It's like she's trying to get him back with these little gestures."

Alice tilted her head in thought. "Have you talked to him about it?"

"Barely," she said, exasperated. "He claims that he's sent her away from Giant's. But who knows? He told me they were engaged and that she was the one who broke things off. I like him, but I'm still processing all of that."

Beth leaned forward, her eyes sparkling with a hint of mischief. "Well, have you tried fighting fire with fire?"

April frowned, confused. "What do you mean?"

"I mean," Beth said, her voice low and sultry, "what if you actually fight her. Like physically. Show her you mean business. I'll bet you could win a fistfight."

The ladies laughed. "Ah, very funny," April said, sarcastically. It hit too close to home for her. Because though she wasn't going to physically fight Lily, she was in the middle of some kind of battle. Half of it was with herself.

Kellie leaned forward and set her wine glass on the table. "You know what? Don't take this the wrong way, April, but I think you should give him an ultimatum. Either he tells Lily to stay away, or you'll leave." The other women nodded in agreement.

April's stomach clenched with anxiety. She had never been one for ultimatums. It always puts unneeded pressure on relationships.

Alice, ever the optimist, winked at her. "Hey, don't worry," she said. "All men are ridiculous. Isn't that why we get together? God invented wine, so we can do just this. Sit here and complain about men."

The four women raised their glasses and clinked them together. But as April sipped, she wondered if any of the suggestions she'd gotten were viable options for her. Probably not. Fist fights and ultimatums. Was that the best she could do for her relationship?

"Okay, can we talk for a minute about how frustrating it is when they leave the toilet seat up?" Kellie began.

The three other women stared at each other. "Yeah, um... None of us are in the position to have a man in our bathroom," April replied as the others burst into laughter.

"The only reason a man would ever be in my pristine bathroom is to fix the faucet," Alice said, raising her glass again.

"Ha, ha, guys. Yes. I sometimes let my boyfriend use my bathroom," Kellie retorted.

Beth clasped her chest as she keeled over in laughter. "Do you have to get your toilet detailed after? Like a car?"

The women couldn't stop laughing. It brought a light to April's dark week thus far. Everything could be going wrong and at least she would have ladies night.

As the night went on and the wine continued to flow, April couldn't help but feel a sense of relief washing over her. It was nice to have a group of girlfriends to vent to and confide in. She had been struggling to keep her emotions in check ever since Lily had entered the picture.

Though her friends didn't provide much clarity on her relationship, they provided April colored glasses. And the reminder that no matter what happened between Nigel and April, she had friends in town.

As the night went on, the laughter subsided, and April headed back to her house, waving goodbye to her friends. Tomorrow was finally time to face reality and all the problems that brought with it.

CHAPTER TWELVE

April awoke early the next morning, determined to start making progress on her project. Though it was chilly outside, she still felt a sense of clarity as she stepped out of her house.

With a wheelbarrow, shovel, and rake in hand, April began weeding the tall grass that had grown around the barn.

She moved diligently, taking her time to clear the area. As she worked, April began to feel a sense of satisfaction coursing through her veins. Her body felt alive with energy, and for a few moments, she was able to forget all her previous worries.

She felt a sense of peace and fulfillment as she toiled away, her hands dirty with soil and sweat dripping from her brow.

As she took a break, leaning against the fence and taking in her work, she was quickly taken aback by looking at the bigger picture. Her portion of the weeded grass was much smaller than she imagined when she was working on it.

At this rate, it would take her much longer than she anticipated. It would take over a year for someone to clean up this ranch area to working condition. Her project was far from complete, and she had so much work ahead of her.

April was so caught up in her thoughts that she didn't even notice the figure standing at the edge of the property. The tall shadow of a man stared at her from afar before slowly approaching.

A chill ran down her spine as she watched him. Who was this man? What did he want?

She took another sip of water before the man came out of the shadows.

As the man drew closer, April could see his rugged features and broad shoulders. His hair was unkempt and his clothes were worn, as if he had been working outside for quite a while.

His brown overalls were covered with dirt and sand, and his boots were scuffed. The man smells of pine and sweat. The sour tang of old sweat. His boots crunched the loose twigs as he stepped closer.

"Jackson," the man said softly, and tipped his hat out to her. "Do I have the pleasure of speaking to April?"

April was hesitant, unsure of who this stranger was and what he wanted. He seemed so serious, focused on only her, as if nothing existed around them.

"Yes, I'm April."

Jackson stepped closer to her, his eyes scanning her face with keen interest. He seemed to be sizing her up as if he was analyzing her. It made April feel uncomfortable, like a lab rat under a microscope.

"Nice to meet you. I've heard a lot of good things," Jackson said.

April couldn't help but feel a sense of unease as Jackson continued to stare at her. She could feel his eyes piercing through her as if he was trying to read her mind. "You've heard good things about me?" she asked, confused.

Jackson smiled shyly. "Yes, from your friend Beth. She was telling people at the diner about your plans to make this place into a horse ranch. Is that not the case anymore?"

She'd forgotten what a small town she lived in, how everybody knew everybody else's business.

Beth was always a bit of a gossip. It didn't mean she wouldn't trust her friend. Beth knew when not to spill the beans. But April thought her big plans may need to be kept closer to her chest from now on.

"No, that's still my plan," April replied, her unease turning into curiosity. "Why do you ask?"

As his eyes darted away from hers, he hesitated. "Well, I might be able to help you with that. I have experience with horses and ranching, and I've been looking for work lately."

April was taken aback by Jackson's offer. She had been so caught up in her own plans that she hadn't even considered the possibility of hiring someone to help her with the ranch side of the property.

"That's quite an offer, Jackson," April said, her eyes lighting up with excitement. "What kind of experience do you have with horses?"

He leaned against the fence, the muscles in his arms flexing as he crossed them over his chest. "I've worked with horses for most of my life. Grew up on a ranch out in Montana. I know how to train them, and I've done just about every job there is on a ranch."

April waited for him to continue his experience, maybe tell her a few stories about his time in Montana, but he didn't. He simply stared back at her, waiting for her response.

"I appreciate the offer, but I don't even know you. How do I know I can trust you?" April asked, her voice laced with caution.

Jackson's expression turned serious. "I understand your concerns, April. But I can assure you that I'm an honest man, just looking for an opportunity to do what I love. I'll work hard and prove to you that you can trust me."

Unsure of what to do, April studied him for a moment. But she could see the determination in his eyes and knew he was serious about wanting to help her. They discussed wages, a description of the most urgent work needed, and his skill set.

After a deep breath, her mind raced as she processed Jackson's offer. She knew the property needed work before she could even begin to think about getting horses. There were debris and broken items scattered around the ranch that would need to be cleared away.

And like she was just considering, it would take her years to do on her own. She was going to need help if this would be a reality.

"Alright," April said after a long pause, "I'll give you a chance. I'll hire you temporarily until we can get this place cleared up and make sure it's ready for renovations."

A smile broke across Jackson's face as he ran his hand through his hair. He seemed relieved at her answer and thanked her with a nod.

"I'll be here first thing in the morning," he said, walking away from her and back into the forest.

April still wasn't sure what direction he'd come from. Hopefully, he lived nearby, so she wouldn't have to worry about him walking to and from the large estate each day.

April watched him go with a feeling of hope swelling up inside her. She may have just found the help she needed to bring her ranching dream to life.

Thoughts crept into her as she began to weed the tall grass yet again. There was still so much more to Jackson that she didn't know. April knew that only time would tell what kind of help Jackson could offer.

But one thing was certain, she thought to herself, there was something very mysterious about him.

CHAPTER THIRTEEN

Staring at her phone screen, April wondered if she should be calling Nigel at this hour. It was right at dinner time when everyone would be at his restaurant. He was probably busy, but she pushed 'call' anyways.

The phone rang five times before she heard the familiar voice recording. This time, she decided to leave a message. At least she knew that they were on okay terms now.

"Hey, I'm just calling to check in. I'm sure it's the dinner rush, but maybe we can talk later."

It was simple and perfect, so she hit 'end call' and stared at her phone screen again.

She sat on her bed, scrolling through social media until she saw something that made her smile. Georgia was surrounded by new friends in the park at a study session.

The photo was captioned, 'Study in the yard'. April wasn't quite sure what that meant, but she couldn't help smiling at the face on the screen. She missed her daughter more than anything.

In fact, it was probably time for a call. She opened Facetime and video called Georgia, waiting to see that beautiful face on her screen again.

As the call connected, April's heart skipped a beat as she saw her daughter's face fill the screen. Georgia's vibrant smile lit up the room, and April couldn't help but feel a sense of pride swell inside her.

"Hi, Mom!" Georgia exclaimed, waving at the camera. "I miss you so much!"

April couldn't help but smile back, feeling her eyes well up with tears. "I miss you too, honey. How's school going?"

"It's going well! I'm keeping up with the work and making some friends. But I wish you were here," Georgia said, her voice tinged with sadness.

"That's sweet, but you'll see me in no time."

Behind her daughter, she saw the typical college dorm room with a desk, large bed, and a closet with a mirror. Bright lights from the street outside cast a pale glow through the thin curtains, leaving the room in a hazy glow.

April couldn't help but feel a sense of nostalgia wash over her. It seemed like just yesterday that she was in college, studying hard and making new friends. Now, her daughter was getting that same experience.

Though, she was slightly afraid just months ago that Georgia would never experience higher education. When her daughter was helping her reimagine the property she laid in now, April never imagined that she would end up back at school learning about interior design.

"Oh, and mom," Georgia began, putting up a hand and getting wide eyed. She was gearing up to tell a story. "You will never guess what this professor did to me the other day."

"What?" April asked, eagerly.

"So, we were talking about color palettes for a design project, and I suggested using a certain shade of blue. And he looked at me and said, 'I'm sorry, I didn't realize Smurfs were in charge of this project,'" Georgia said, rolling her eyes.

April let out a chuckle. "That's awful, but kind of funny."

The two talked about her time at school for the next half hour. April listened intently as Georgia vented about the ins and outs of her life.

As their conversation slowed, April couldn't help but feel a sense of pride and satisfaction. Her daughter was thriving in college and pursuing her passions, just as she had always hoped.

"Well, I've been having an interesting week here, too."

"Oh, really?" Georgia replied, spreading herself across her bed and kicking her feet in the air behind her. "Tell me about it."

April explained about the guest who left early and the ones who might have stolen something from her. Then she talked just a little about Nigel.

Georgia knew who Nigel was and that she was starting to date again. But she refused to give too many details about her love life to her daughter. Some things were meant to be more private.

The only detail she gave away was that they were on the rocks after his ex came into town, despite Nigel saying he wanted to be with April.

"Hm, that is a weird situation. I wish I could give you advice, but my only serious boyfriend was in high school. And we both know how that turned out."

The boy was nice, but their chemistry was never off the charts. They broke up after a few months.

Just as April was about to say goodbye, a knock came to her door. Even Georgia's brows furrowed. "Hold on," she told her daughter. "Come in!"

Richard's head slipped into the doorway. "Hey, hun. How's it going? I'm just checking in."

"Oh, it's your grandfather," April said to the phone. "I'm talking to Georgia, if you want to come say hi."

The smile that Richard's face grew was wide and bright. He almost couldn't believe it as he stepped into the room. "I'd be delighted." He marveled at the sight of his granddaughter on the other side of the screen.

April was glad he had the opportunity to see her. They'd barely known each other growing up. Because of his frequent absences, her father wasn't around enough for Georgia to really remember him.

"Hey, sweetheart," he said to the screen.

Georgia smiled softly and waved a hand. "Hi, how are you?"

Her mood had completely shifted from when she was just speaking with her mother. It was more subdued, cautious, as if she was talking to a stranger.

"I'm doing well, hun. How are you doing over there? I hear you're studying?"

Georgia looked off screen and nodded her head. "I'm doing well, studying hard! But uh... I actually have to run. My friends are having a little get-together. Mom, I'll call you again soon, okay?"

"Okay, love. Sounds good," April said, waving to the screen. "Be safe! Talk to you later!"

The screen went black as the call ended. "She's grown so much," Richard said.

April nodded. "She has. A full grown adult now."

It was clear they both knew the situation was uncomfortable. Her daughter had left so abruptly that it was obvious something was weird between them all. She couldn't tell her father that his own granddaughter definitely didn't want to speak with him.

So they all just pretended like everything was fine.

"Well, I just came in to say goodnight," Richard said as he walked back to the door.

"Thanks, dad. Have a good night. You're comfortable in your room?" April crossed her fingers that he would say yes. After all of his requests and changes, all she needed was for him to not complain for five minutes.

He nodded. "Yeah, ever since I got those new pillows I sleep great!"

Oh, great. The pillows again. At least he didn't have anything new to complain about.

"Good, I'm glad. Goodnight," April said as she watched him leave the room.

Once Richard was out of sight, April got up to tidy her room.

She straightened the sheets, fluffed the pillows, and picked up a few items that had been left out of place. As she worked, her mind wandered back to her conversation with Georgia.

She couldn't help but feel a sense of pride and joy for her daughter. Georgia was thriving in college and pursuing her passions, just as April had hoped. It was a relief to see her daughter happy and successful, especially after all they had been through.

As April began to set up her nightstand with her phone charger, she realized something was missing. Behind her small lamp, she always had her small blue elephant figurine. It was another one of the thrift store finds, except this time it was from years ago.

She'd picked it up at an expo after Georgia was born. It had some kind of sentimental value to it, but April knew she could live without looking at it each night. It was just strange that it was now lost when she knew she had it the night before.

April searched the room for the small figurine, but it was nowhere to be found. She checked under the bed, in the drawers, and even in the closet, but to no avail. It had simply vanished.

She sighed and sat down on her bed, trying to think of where else it might have gone. Maybe she'd taken it out of the room without remembering? Or maybe someone had moved it without her noticing?

She even checked the bathroom, but it was not there either. She couldn't shake the feeling that something was off.

She frowned, feeling a pang of worry in her chest.

Had she misplaced it somewhere else? Or did someone take it?

The thought of someone stealing from her made her feel uneasy. She shook her head, trying to shrug off the feeling. It was just a small trinket, after all.

But then, a different thought crossed her mind. Could it have been her father?

He was just in her room. One of the few who had access to it. And he did walk away when she was talking about the Millers, whose room happened to be missing a trinket as well.

She quickly dismissed the thought, not wanting to think this way about her own father. But she couldn't help but wonder if Richard had something to do with the recent thefts.

No, it couldn't be him. That didn't make sense. What would her father have to gain from taking small objects from around the house? It's not like they were from when he lived here. They were completely April's.

He wouldn't steal from his own daughter, would he?

April shook her head, trying to push the thought aside. She decided to focus on the positive, like the fact that Georgia was doing well in school, and her father seemed to be content with his new pillows.

It was the simple things in life, wasn't it?

However, as she lay in bed, her mind kept wandering back to the missing figurine. She couldn't shake the feeling that it left a bad taste in her mouth.

April closed her eyes and tried to clear her mind. She took a deep breath and exhaled slowly, trying to calm her racing thoughts.

So much was happening in her life. Did she have to add this to the list too? Watching out for thieves in the night? And becoming a detective to solve the case of the missing elephant figurine and jewelry box?

At this point, who knew what tomorrow would bring. She thought about that as she slowly fell asleep.

CHAPTER FOURTEEN

"Thanks, Millie," April called out from the doorway into the bed and breakfast. "I'll be back in a little while."

April wore a pair of denim overalls that fit tight around her form. The pocket had a flowery emblem and the pockets were big enough to fit her small gardening tools. On her waist, she wrapped a red bandana around the loop of her belt. It was soft from washing and many uses. Its edges were frayed, but she folded it in half to make it more managcable.

In her hands she held her normal tools, a rake and bucket for the weeds.

As she walked out to the barn, she saw Jackson, her recently hired ranch hand. He was wearing a pair of faded jeans, a plaid shirt, and boots that had seen better days. His brown hair was pushed away from his face, revealing his strong features.

He'd already done more than April had been able to get done in two days of work. And his section of the grass already looked much bettcr than the one she was working on. How long had he been out here today already?

For a moment, she just sat back and watched his technique. If they were going to get this done, she would need to learn to be as efficient as he was.

"Good morning, Jackson," April called out to him with a friendly wave.

He turned around and smiled at her. "Morning, April. Ready to get to work?"

April nodded with a determined look on her face. "Yes, let's get these weeds out of here."

She set her tools down beside him and began digging up the horridly overgrown plants where she had left off the day before.

The two worked side by side in companionable silence. April enjoyed the peaceful moment, and was grateful for Jackson's help. It was almost like they had been working together for years, not days.

The sun shone brightly down on them as they labored away, and April felt a sense of contentment begin to wash over her. The air was filled with the smell of freshly cut grass and dirt, and the bright yellow birds sang sweetly in the swaying trees above them.

As time passed, they worked side by side without speaking much but still understanding each other perfectly. April found herself getting lost in the sounds of nature around her as Jackson's movements became mesmerizingly familiar.

Occasionally, one of them would stop to wipe their brow or take a drink from their water bottle before plunging back into their work with renewed vigor.

Just over an hour had passed when April was startled by a loud noise near the forest. The whinny of a large horse and heavy feet stomping on the ground.

Jackson and April looked at each other before rushing over to the animal. As soon as she saw it, she knew it was injured.

They approached cautiously, being mindful of the poor animal's space. It clamored its hoof against the ground, like a human stepping foot on a loose lego.

Jackson slowly stepped forward, getting low to try and check out its front right foot.

April stayed back, watching him intently. She could see the muscles in his back tense as he reached out to touch the horse's leg. She held her breath, waiting for him to report back to her.

"There's something lodged in there. It's some kind of metal post. If he stomps on it too much, it'll get too deep and really hurt him. I have to get it out while we still can," Jackson said, keeping completely still so not to scare the horse.

April couldn't believe what she was hearing. Of course, she wanted to help the animal, but she would have had no clue what to do in this situation. Her first instinct would have been to call animal control to help the helpless horse out.

"Are you sure we should be doing that?"

Jackson nodded. "Yes. It'll be alright. Just watch him for me. I'm going to get closer."

April watched nervously as Jackson slowly approached the horse, making soft, soothing sounds to calm it down. She could see the sweat glistening on his forehead as he knelt down beside the animal's leg and began to examine it more closely.

As he got closer, the horse began to relax, and Jackson was able to get a better look at the metal post that was lodged in its foot. Thankfully, from afar anyway, it looked like it hadn't hit anything important. It was stuck in a small portion of its hoof and scraped up the front of the shin.

It could have been much worse from the sound of it.

Carefully, Jackson began to touch the animal to get a feel for it. The animal began to breathe heavy and kicked its front leg just in front of Jackson.

"Careful," April said aloud in a neutral tone, making sure not to spook the tall wild horse.

April could see the determination in Jackson's eyes as he worked, his hands moving with incredible precision. It was clear that he had experience with this sort of thing, and she couldn't help but feel grateful that he was here to help.

Finally, with a soft grunt, Jackson was able to extract the post completely. He held it up triumphantly, and the horse let out a relieved whinny.

After backing up quickly, he threw the metal in the bucket beside the barn and watched the horse begin to buck around the trees.

April couldn't help but be impressed by his skills. If she wasn't so interested in Nigel, she would have been taken by him completely.

As the horse galloped away, April turned to Jackson with a look of gratitude in her eyes. "Thank you so much for your help. I wouldn't have known what to do without you."

Jackson shrugged modestly. "It's no problem. Just doing my job." He flashed her a smile that made her heart skip a beat.

April couldn't help but admire him even more for his humility. It was clear that he was a man who knew his strengths but didn't feel the need to show them off unnecessarily.

It was hard not to admire the handsome, mysterious man in front of her. Especially when things had been so rocky with Nigel. Did that mean it was okay to look at Jackson like she was now? With such admiration?

She shook off the feelings as they walked back to the front of the barn, where the weeds were waiting for them.

But that's not all that was waiting there. An older woman with a clipboard at her side was walking through the property. She wore a pantsuit, less fancy than the ones in April's closet that she used to wear to court. But still professional-looking nonetheless.

April swallowed hard and looked over at a confused Jackson. He shrugged his shoulders and got back to work. She liked that he knew when to mind his own business.

As the woman approached them, April could see that she had a stern expression on her face. She straightened her posture and put on her best professional demeanor.

"Good afternoon," the woman said, her voice firm and commanding. "I need to know what you're doing to this land."

It wasn't a question. It was a clear statement. "We're cleaning it up. Who wants to know?" April responded, annoyed at the woman's tone.

She tried to recall if there was anything she hadn't done properly. Was there something wrong with clearing out the debris in a two-hundred-acre property with your name on it?

"I'm Trisha. I come from the island's council. I've been sent to talk to you about your intentions on this ranch."

Now April was thoroughly annoyed. "My intentions? Why is that any of your business?"

The snooty woman crossed her arms in front of her chest, the clipboard clanging against her chunky necklace. "Because you need permits. Lots of them. And once you get permission for the permits, you'll need to file an intent to change the zoning. Technically, all two hundred acres here are residential. So if you plan on making this into a commercial horse ranch, you're going to need to jump through a lot of hoops."

April had just begun the process of cleaning up the areas she wanted to transform. She knew that there would be paperwork, but what this woman was describing was so much more than she expected.

"Wait a minute, how did you even know I wanted to turn this into a horse ranch? Maybe I'm using it for residential purposes. Can't people have yards anymore?"

Even Jackson's head turned at her comment. It would have to be an extremely large yard, but it could be a yard. Unfortunately for April it wasn't. But she wasn't about to show all of her cards to this woman who intruded on her property.

She chuckled. "Listen, April. We've heard the rumors. Everyone in town is aware of what you're trying to do."

"You have no idea what I'm trying to do."

Trisha looked past her to Jackson, pulling weeds. The only thing April could do was keep her face. If she faltered, Trisha would win. "Right. We could make a few educated guesses, and we're nervous about your ideas."

April gritted her teeth. She hated small towns and the way everyone seemed to know everything about everyone else's business. "Well, I haven't submitted any paperwork yet. So technically, I haven't done anything wrong."

Trisha raised an eyebrow. "That may be true. But I suggest you get started on those permits and paperwork as soon as possible. And don't even think about starting any construction until you have the proper approvals."

With that, Trisha turned on her heel and walked away, leaving April seething with anger. April sighed heavily, feeling relieved that the unpleasant encounter was finally over. But at the same time, she was overwhelmed by all the new information that had just been thrown at her.

This town was trying to stop her from creating this horse ranch even before she had begun building it.

CHAPTER FIFTEEN

April sat on Alice's deck beside the beach with a coffee mug in her left hand and her phone in her right. "Do you know about these rumors? About me doing the horse ranch thing?"

Alice raised her brows. "Is it really a rumor if it's right?"

The rumor was right, but April didn't like that her plans were getting around town. "I mean, yes, because I didn't tell all of those people. Now, the city is asking questions. This is why I never listen to gossip." She shook her head and took another sip of her warm coffee.

The sky was a light blue, with fluffy clouds floating by intermittently. The sun was just over the horizon, sending bright red beams of light at various angles across the water.

Tastes of salt and coffee mix on her tongue and created something beautiful in the late morning air. The small waves crashed onto the shore and threatened to rise to the deck that never seemed to get wet.

"Well, I have a rumor you might be interested in knowing," Alice said, brows raised and a smirk across her face.

April leaned forward in her chair. "Tell me everything."

She wasn't keen on gossip, unless of course the rumors were about anyone other than herself. Then and only then did she absolutely love it. Besides, she needed to know what was going on in town to figure out what to do next. Why was the city after her when she hadn't done anything wrong?

Alice leaned in, looking both ways as if someone was going to surprise them and listen in. "I've heard that Isaac Greenfield is running for mayor. One of the first times there's been someone so young."

Young was an interesting way to put it. He was fifty-one and still chipper as ever. April knew that he owned a few buildings in town. He was remarkably wealthy, but that was about all she knew about him.

She shrugged. "What does that have to do with my problem?"

"He's running to try and 'modernize' the island."

Alice's brows raised, and she held out her hands. April still didn't understand. "Which means..."

After a few seconds of waiting, Alice let out a big sigh. "He's trying to take away your horses. The wild horses on the island? He wants

65

them out. Says that it'll become a safety hazard once they put in a highway and all these other tourist attractions. He was spewing all these reasons the horses need to go."

April's heart sank. She had always admired the wild horses on the island. It was a part of her childhood. And what about her plans to incorporate them into her horse ranch? What would her ranch be without any horses to help?

If Isaac Greenfield was successful in his campaign, it would mean the end of her horse ranch plans as well.

The wild horses on the island were a part of its charm, its history.

"That's ridiculous. The wild horses have been here for centuries. They're a part of the island's identity," April said, her voice laced with anger and frustration.

"I know, but you know how these politicians are. They only care about their own interests," Alice said, shaking her head. "I'm sorry, April."

April sighed, feeling defeated. She had already been dealing with the city council's permits.

Things were beginning to get extremely hard. April didn't have unlimited finances. It was hard enough to save money for the renovations, and now she was employing two people to help her. How would she ever have enough money to pay for the permits, inspections, and all of the fees that came with the bureaucracy?

Sitting back in her chair, April stared out at the ocean. She felt trapped and helpless. "What am I going to do?" she muttered.

Isaac was definitely the one who sent the town hall after her. Who else would have the influence and motive to try and shut down a horse ranch that hadn't even started renovations or paperwork?

It made sense. He didn't want horses here, and April was literally building them a refuge.

She felt a knot form in her stomach as she thought about the possibility of losing the wild horses and the impact it would have on her own plans. But she wasn't going to let Isaac Greenfield take away something so integral to the island's history without a fight.

Alice put a hand on her shoulder. "We'll figure something out. Don't worry."

"I have to go to town hall and figure out a way to get them off my back. They want my paperwork when I don't even know what I'm doing yet. It's impossible."

April couldn't help but feel a sense of determination wash over her. She wasn't going to give up on her dream of creating a horse ranch on the island, and she definitely wasn't going to let Isaac Greenfield or anyone else take away the wild horses that had been a part of the island's identity for centuries.

She was going to have to fight for what she believed in, no matter the cost.

***

As April walked downtown, she contemplated her next move. The streets bustled around her as she kept her head down in thought.

The streets were packed with tourists. There were shops in every direction, selling memorabilia from the past and present. The shops lined the streets and stretched out for blocks. Every shop she passed had something new to offer.

It was all a reminder that tourist season would be well underway soon enough.

April felt the sun warm her as she walked. The cool breeze put a chill up her back. Still, she kept walking forward, the only way to figure out what to do next.

On her way to the town hall, she saw the sign that always put a lump in her throat. Giant's.

Nigel was inside that burger joint. She wanted to see him so badly, to tell him everything that was going on. Aside from Alice, he was one of the people she felt like she could tell anything to. At least, he was before Lily showed up and threw a wrench in things.

April thought that it was better that she showed up now instead of in a few years when things were really getting serious between them. At least Nigel was being forced to confront things now when it was easier.

She took a deep breath and opened the door to Giant's. Nigel sat behind the counter, wearing his usual smile. He looked up when he heard the bell ring, and their eyes met.

Nigel stopped what he was doing and stepped out from behind the counter. He walked over to her and gave her a gentle hug. April felt herself relax in his arms, as if nothing had happened at all.

"How are you?" he asked, seemingly happier than ever.

April was surprised that he ignored the other customers in his restaurant. No one stared, they were occupied with their own conversations. But still, it was a display of affection in front of everyone who knew he owned the place.

"There's so much going on," April admitted, head down. "I'm honestly so confused at this point. It feels like everything is against me."

Nigel nodded along as she spoke. "I get it. I'm sorry things seem to be so crazy for you right now."

He motioned for her to follow him, taking his seat behind the counter again. The stool at the very corner was the only quiet spot open, so April sat there, looking deeply at the handsome man before her.

His chiseled face and dark eyes captivated her. She felt a pang of guilt for thinking that way when she had so much on her plate, but she couldn't help herself. Nigel was attractive, and she had always been drawn to him.

"Look, I wanted to say I'm really sorry about last night. I saw your call and I should have picked up," Nigel explained, head hung low. "Honestly, I should have run over to the house and talked to you in person."

April wondered why he didn't. What was he so busy with that he couldn't take a phone call? Or was it because he didn't want to talk to her?

Trying to play it cool, she shrugged. "I understand."

She'd already interrogated him enough lately. It was time to settle it down. She just wanted her friend back, her favorite person to talk to. Then slowly they could uncover their feelings, just like they'd been playing to do all along.

It was supposed to go slow. It's just that Lily's arrival left them at a standstill.

"Maybe I could do something for you tonight, to make up for it?" His eyes twinkled, and his smirk made her heart race.

The bell sounded behind them, but neither paid attention, too encapsulated by the discussion at hand.

It wasn't until Lily's hand was on the bar top that April even noticed she'd walked in. As soon as she saw it, a chill went up her spine. Not just out of fear of what would happen next, but out of anger and jealousy.

April looked to Nigel for his reaction. Clearly, he wasn't as bothered as her. But he didn't look happy to see Lily either. It was more like indifference.

"Hey, Nigel," Lily said, her voice low and sultry. She leaned across the bar, as if April wasn't there at all. "It was great to see you last night."

April couldn't believe what she'd just heard. So much in fact that she wondered if Lily had spoken at all. Had she imagined it?

But then she looked up at Nigel, who stared at her wide-eyed. "April, that's not... It's not what you..."

Without another word, April stood and walked out of the restaurant. Even in the fresh air, she felt like she could barely breathe. Though no one was looking at her, she could see the eyes of everyone in town staring.

Her hand clasped onto her chest. All she could do was walk. One step after another. She had to focus only on that.

As she walked, her thoughts raced. How could Nigel do this to her? Had he been seeing Lily behind her back? She thought that she was crazy for thinking that was true. But now, she was confronted with the fact that she was right all along.

Tears streamed down her face as she walked aimlessly through the streets. April walked and walked, the wind whipping her hair around her face. Her mind was racing, trying to process what she had just seen and heard.

When she finally reached her car, her hand on the handle, Nigel called out behind her. "Wait! April, please," he cried.

April turned around, her eyes red and puffy from crying. "What do you want?" she asked, her voice breaking. "What could you possibly have to say to me?"

Nigel approached her, his expression pleading. "Please, let me explain. That wasn't what it looked like."

"That's the best you've got?" April replied, trying not to scream it out for the entire town to hear.

When Nigel didn't continue pleading, she slid into her car and slammed the door shut. Nothing else he could say in that moment would have made her feel better.

Instead of answering her call, he was off with his ex-girlfriend doing God knows what. Just thinking about it made her want to sob.

April drove around town, not knowing where she was going. The scenery passed her by in a blur, her thoughts lost in a sea of confusion and pain. She couldn't believe that Nigel, someone she trusted, would betray her like this.

Her grip on the steering wheel tightened as she thought of Lily and Nigel together. The thought made her sick to her stomach.

She drove until she reached a quiet beach, where the waves crashed against the shore. April parked the car and got out, taking off her shoes and walking towards the water.

The sand was warm beneath her feet, and the water was cold and refreshing. April walked until the water reached her ankles, then stood there, watching the waves come and go.

She knew that she was heading to the town hall next, but she needed to think.

Everything felt like it was falling apart. She wanted to give herself one moment where she could wipe her tears away and pull it together.

Because once she walked into that hall, she was going to give them a piece of her mind. And she needed her frustration to do that.

The devastation of the news of Lily and Nigel wasn't fueling her fire, but dampening it. It made her want to cry and scream instead of fight.

And right now, April needed to fight.

CHAPTER SIXTEEN

The only sound in the town hall was April's steps echoing off the empty walls.

The town hall was an old building built in the early 1900s.

The wooden floor creaked softly under her weight, but didn't give way, and the grey walls were dirty from years of grime. The hall was a bit dusty and smelled like old books.

What surprised her the most was the lack of signs pointing to the different departments and conference rooms. She got lost more than once on her way to the receptionist's desk for the town council.

"Is this where I might find council woman Trisha?" April asked as she approached the small woman with glasses.

She was a small woman with curly brown hair and glittering green eyes. Her smile was warm and welcoming as she looked up to greet April.

"Yes, you're in the right place. How may I help you today, hun?"

With adrenaline in her veins, April's words tumbled out of her mouth. "I need to speak with her or another member of the council immediately."

"What is this regarding?" the woman said, clicking away on her keyboard with a smile.

April was almost annoyed with the optimism of the receptionist. "It's regarding my property. Trisha gave me a visit yesterday, so she should know what I'm talking about."

"Do you have an appointment?" she asked with a smile, taking a break from her keyboard to look up at April.

"No, but I need information regarding permits, fees and inspections."

The woman's smile faltered slightly at April's tone, but she quickly recovered. "I see. Well, let me see if I can schedule a meeting for you."

April nodded, trying to calm down her nerves. She knew that she had to keep her cool if she wanted to make any progress.

"Unfortunately, there's no available appointments for today. But I can see if anyone's available to talk to you."

April watched as the woman picked up the phone and dialed a number, her mind racing with all the things she needed to say to the council. She needed to make sure that her questions were answered.

After a few moments, the receptionist hung up the phone and turned to April. "Councilman Rodriguez will see you now. His office is down the hall, last door on the right."

"Thank you."

When she reached the door, she took a deep breath and knocked. "Come in," a gruff voice said from inside.

April opened the door and stepped inside, her eyes immediately drawn to the man sitting behind the desk. He was a middle-aged man with a thick mustache and a stern expression.

"Please, have a seat," he said, gesturing to the chair in front of his desk. April sat in the uncomfortable wooden seat opposite of him. "How can I help you today?"

She took a deep breath. There was so much to say, but she needed to be articulate. April knew she couldn't give them any reason to doubt her. Eventually, they would need to approve her paperwork.

"I'm not sure if you heard, but Trisha came by and told me that I needed some permits," she said, as sweetly as she possibly could. April knew that everyone at town hall knew about her and her situation.

But if she was going to get her information, she had to play dumb. She needed to act as though everything was fine.

"Oh, of course." Rodriguez got out every step of paperwork April would have to go through in order to make her two hundred acre property into a working horse ranch.

She listened intently, jotting down notes as he spoke. And asked clarifying questions when necessary, making sure she understood all the steps and fees involved.

"And is there any law against me cleaning up my property? Even with the current buildings, like the barn?"

She knew the answer. Her law degree might have been collecting dust for the moment, but she knew how to read the island's rules regarding property.

What she was looking for was for the councilman to admit that she wasn't breaking any law by continuing to clean up her property.

With the amount of hoops they seemed to want her to jump through, April was sure that she would have to deny any talk of her horse ranch. For now, at least. Once she had all of the plans, then she would apply for the permits.

It was a setback for sure, but at least she'd be able to continue her work without people questioning her every move.

Rodriguez looked nervous. "No, of course not. But if there are plans in place to"

"There aren't any current plans," April interrupted with a knowing smile. "But I do appreciate the information on the laws and regulations. I'll make sure to remember them as I consider what to do with my empty property."

Rising to leave, April collected her notebook and put it back in her purse.

As she walked towards the door, she turned back to the councilman. "Thank you for your time, Councilman Rodriguez. I'll be sure to follow the procedures outlined."

She flashed him a smile and walked out of the room, closing the door behind her.

As she walked back down the hallway, April couldn't help but feel a sense of relief wash over her. She had the information she needed to move forward with her plans for the horse ranch, and she knew exactly what steps she needed to take next.

Unfortunately for her, those steps involved convincing everyone that she wasn't planning to run a horse ranch on her property. Which meant that she had a lot of work ahead of her before she was even able to begin thinking about the necessary renovations for the barn and other outbuildings.

It was a setback, for sure. But one that April thought gave her a chance at making this a reality.

Just as April was about to walk out of the building, a man stepped inside. He wore a nice suit and carried a briefcase, his grey hair combed neatly back from his face.

The receptionist from before welcomed him into the building. "Good afternoon, Mister Greenfield."

April stopped in her tracks and looked at the man. He was wearing a dark grey suit and had an air of authority about him that made her heart skip a beat.

"Isaac Greenfield?" April said aloud, taking her hand off of the door to turn and face him.

This was the same man who was trying to take her down. He was the one who made Trisha come out to her property. He was trying to take the horses away from the island.

Everything that had happened so far made her braver than ever. Her anger pushed her forward, willing her to say whatever she wanted to this man she recently found out was her true enemy. They were on opposing sides of this little war, and neither knew would exist until recently.

April thought of her returning father, who only pointed out everything wrong. She thought of Nigel, who was talking to his ex-girlfriend and not telling her a single thing about it. And she thought of this man in front of her, who wanted to take down her dreams. The man who wanted to push out the animals she loved from the only home they'd ever known.

"Yes?" he said, smiling at her.

She was sure that he had no idea what was about to hit him. "My name is April Faith. You're the man who's running for mayor?"

Her adrenaline was pumping faster than it had ever been before. All of her frustrations

Walking away from the receptionist desk and getting just a foot away from April, he replied, "Yes, I am. And it's nice to finally put a face to the name."

"So you know why I'm here. You sent someone out to my property to tell me I needed a hundred permits."

Her voice was low, so not to alert everyone around to their discussion.

"Because you do need them. Or... You will need them when you create this little ranch of yours. It's quite a few hoops to jump through if you ask me."

April rolled her eyes. "Yeah, right. You're not trying to make me do paperwork. You're trying to put a stop to-"

He stopped her with a hand up between them.

It made April even more furious that he would interrupt her like that. She was taken aback by his audacity, just as she was about to go off on him, he was stopping her.

Isaac smirked and leaned in closer. "I know exactly what I'm doing here, okay? You don't have to tell me my plans. Because I made the plans myself. And they're good plans."

She was astounded by his confidence, his direct attitude, like he was clearly gunning for her and was upset that she didn't back down. It was arrogance if she'd ever seen it.

April felt her blood boil as she stared at Isaac. This man was clearly not someone to be tangled with.

After everything she'd been through, she knew she couldn't let him intimidate her. She could feel her anger boiling inside of her, and she knew that she had to be careful with her words if she wanted to come out on top of this confrontation.

She whispered, trying to sound just as sure of herself. "They're not going to work. Because I'm just cleaning out my property. Nothing you can do to stop that."

The man scoffed in her face. "Yeah, right. Sure you are. All I'm saying is if I was you, I'd be doing things differently."

April's eyes narrowed at Isaac's words, feeling the fire of determination inside her burn even brighter. After gritting her teeth, she took a deep breath, trying to keep her cool. She wasn't going to let him intimidate her, no matter how confident he seemed to be.

"Lucky for me, you're not me. And what makes you think you know what's best for me? You don't even know me."

"Oh, I know you. I know exactly who you are and what you're trying to do. Just some advice, if I were you, I'd be stripping that land of all its ugly little buildings and subdividing it to corporate interests."

It hit her like a bullet to the stomach. It made her sick to even think about. Her family property being divided and used for money instead of her dreams of making it into a place for the community over all else.

She didn't know what to say. How was she supposed to respond to a man who didn't care? She couldn't magically convince him to care about this island and its people.

"Just know that I'll be here every step of the way. Trust me when I say that I'll make sure every voting citizen of this island knows what's going on here."

She wasn't confident about that, but she sounded like she was, and that was all she needed. April was still relatively new to town. She had no pull with the people here to say who they should or shouldn't vote for.

Whatever she said would be taken with a grain of salt.

"And trust me when I say you don't want to start a war with me, Miss Faith."

April felt a shiver run down her spine at the threat in his voice, but she refused to let him see her fear.

She opened her mouth to continue arguing, but no words came out. The frustration was beginning to get to her. Her cheeks grew hot at the realization that he was winning the argument.

Now he whispered even quieter, bringing his face even closer. "Because decisions about the horrid place you call your property are not up to me, I will continue to pester you until you learn that you do not belong here."

April felt her heart race as Isaac's breath hit her face. She wanted to push him away, to scream at him to leave her alone, but she knew that would only make things worse. Instead, she took a step back, trying to create some distance between them.

Understanding that he won, Isaac stood up straighter. A smile was plastered across his face.

April was seething with anger at Isaac's words, but she refused to let him see her break. This man was a monster, and she couldn't believe he was trying to intimidate her like this. She wouldn't let him win.

Isaac Greenfield walked back towards his office with a smile. "Have a nice day, Mrs. Faith," he called out before he shut the door to the room.

She stood there, speechless and feeling more inadequate than ever.

CHAPTER SEVENTEEN

When April arrived back at the bed and breakfast, she saw her father sitting on one of the benches outside. He had a pleading look in his eyes as he watched her approach.

What could he possibly need now?

"Hey, kiddo," he said with a smile, eyes filled with hope. "I was wondering if you had time to help me with something."

April couldn't help but feel annoyed at her father's request, especially after the confrontation she had just faced. She tried to keep her tone level as she asked, "What do you need help with, Dad?"

"It's just a small errand, really. The fridge is getting pretty empty. I was hoping you could do a grocery store run."

She didn't have the energy to deal with her father's requests right now, but she couldn't bring herself to say no to him either. April's heart sank at the thought of having to run another errand.

April couldn't help but let out a small sigh. "Dad, isn't there enough food in there for a few days?"

Shaking his head, he shrugged. "No, unfortunately. I don't have anything to make my tacos tonight. We need beef and veggies and tortillas."

So basically all of the ingredients for tacos. She knew that there was enough food in there to last him a few days. He specifically wanted tacos and wanted her to be the one to go get the ingredients.

"Fine, I can go grab that for you in a bit," she replied.

Just before April could step foot into the lobby, a dark-haired man walked into the entryway, extremely angry. His thick, bushy eyebrows were turned down and his large mouth was open wide, ready to yell.

"I demand to speak to the owner of this establishment!" he shouted, his voice echoing through the lobby.

April stepped forward, determined to handle the situation. "I'm the owner," she said firmly.

As he looked at April, she realized just how angry he was. And that his suitcase traveled closely behind him. "The people you employ are horrible. This man over here told me that I shouldn't be allowed to heat up my fish in the community kitchen oven."

April looked over at her father, shocked. He shrugged as if nothing significant had happened. "He takes too long in there. If he's going to use the oven for an hour every night and make the whole kitchen smell like fish, I think he should be cooking in a private kitchen."

Wanting to scream but knowing she shouldn't escalate the conversation, she took a few deep breaths. In the time it took her to recollect herself, the two men had already begun arguing again.

"I need fish! My doctor says that it's necessary for my health! It's a health condition! Why couldn't I just use the kitchen for an hour? Every other guest is allowed to use it!"

Richard's face never faltered, it stayed unbothered and annoyed. "Yes, but every other guest doesn't make the whole kitchen smell like Halibut."

"Alright, alright," April said. "Dad, go sit in the lobby please. I'll talk to you in a minute."

He sauntered off into a chair in the middle of the lobby, grunting under his heavy breath.

"I'm so sorry about him. That was obviously uncalled for. You are more than welcome to use any of the facilities. I assure you this will never happen again," she reassured him.

The guest looked her up and down. "I want out. I'm leaving tonight and I want a refund for the nights I'm not staying here."

April felt a knot form in her stomach. Losing a paying customer was never easy, especially when they were leaving on bad terms. "I understand your frustration, but I would really appreciate it if you stayed. We want to accommodate you, so I would be willing to offer you half off the rest of your stay."

It was hard to say because she would be losing so much money on the room. But she knew she had to do something because she wanted him to stay. She wanted this business to thrive, and for that, she needed guests and glowing reviews.

If he stayed, she would have a chance to make it up to him.

He put a hand up to his chin. He actually looked like he was considering her offer. But just when she was feeling good about it, he replied, "No, I just want to leave as soon as possible."

Taking a deep breath, she replied, "I understand. I'll authorize a refund for the remaining nights of your stay."

The man nodded, a satisfied smirk on his face. "Good. And I expect it to be processed immediately."

April nodded, biting her tongue to prevent herself from saying something she'd regret. She walked over to the front desk and began the process of refunding the man's payment.

The guest left immediately, his bags trailing behind him as he wheeled them off to his car. As he drove off, April cursed under her breath. Could this day get any worse?

April typed away until the refund was processed. When she was finally able to look up, she saw Millie talking to her father in the lobby.

"Hey," she began to say, walking over to them. But then she overheard part of their conversation that made her stop in her tracks.

"You're gorgeous, I bet you can get any guy you want," Richard told Millie.

She was half of his age, someone he definitely shouldn't be flirting with, according to his daughter standing right beside him. It was appalling to listen to. A part of her wanted to throw up. But she swallowed her sick stomach to continue.

Millie giggled nervously, clearly uncomfortable with the situation. "Uh, thanks Mr. Johnson. But I'm actually not interested in dating right now."

Richard chuckled, undeterred. "Nonsense! A pretty young thing like you should be out there enjoying life and all it has to offer. Don't waste your youth."

April couldn't take it anymore. "Dad," she said firmly, "we need to talk."

Richard looked up at his daughter, surprised by the interruption. "What is it, sweetie?"

"Millie, could you go check on that room that just left? He's not going to be returning," April said, hoping that she would take the out to leave the uncomfortable conversation. The worker nodded her head and ran off to clean.

April thought about her horrible day. Anger had been building inside of her. She was ready to burst open.

"Dad, what were you thinking?" she said, her voice shaking with rage. "You can't talk to people like that. You can't come in here and ask for my help and then make people leave by arguing with them."

His head sunk. It would have made her feel bad if it wasn't for the fact that all she saw now was red.

"It wasn't my fault. He was the one cooking fish in a shared kitchen. That's a known rule," he said, brows furrowed. April realized that he truly thought he'd done nothing wrong.

He never thought he did anything wrong. That was what April found so infuriating about him. It didn't matter what she said, he would always have an excuse. There was someone or something else to blame.

But April had had enough. Not just with her father, but with everyone. No one seemed to give her a break. Everything she did came with a fight of some kind.

She continued, unable to stop her rants, "And you can't just hit on my employees like that! It's unprofessional and inappropriate."

Richard's face contorted into a confused expression. "What are you talking about, April? I was just giving her a compliment. There's nothing wrong with that. I was just having a little fun. It's not like I'm hurting anyone."

"Can you just please-" she began to cry out, her head in her palms. But her father put a hand out, stopping her in her tracks.

She looked up at his face, waiting for him to respond. Waiting to continue yelling at him for everything he'd done wrong. She needed an outlet for this fury burning inside of her.

"I'm sorry," Richard said. It was the two words she'd been waiting all day to hear. Everyone should have been saying it, but it meant something coming from her father. One apology was better than none.

April wiped her eyes and took a deep breath, trying to calm herself down. She didn't want to fight anymore. She was exhausted.

With a frown and raised brows, he appeared genuinely remorseful, a look of regret etched on his face. It was a rare moment of vulnerability between them.

Though one apology wouldn't make up for everything, it was a start.

When April didn't respond, he continued, "I know that it's been a hard few days. And I wanted to thank you for putting up with me."

April stared at her father, not sure what to make of his sudden change in mood. She had been ready to keep fighting, to keep yelling until she was hoarse, but now... she wasn't so sure.

Maybe it was the exhaustion getting to her, or maybe it was the fact that her father had actually apologized, but for the first time in what felt like forever, she felt herself softening towards him.

"I appreciate your apology, Dad," she said quietly, unsure of how to respond.

April didn't want to admit it, but hearing those words made her feel a little better. Maybe her father wasn't completely hopeless after all.

Her father smiled up at her. "I've really enjoyed being able to spend time together here."

The time they'd spent together was far from perfect. It was nothing like what she expected when he told her that he wanted to make things up to her and rekindle their relationship.

He'd always come when he wanted something. But she always let him, because he was still her dad.

And it was times like this that reminded her of that fact. That people could change, and this time could be different. This could be the time that he actually showed her that he was different now. He hadn't showed any improvement until now, but it was a small step forward.

April didn't believe he was a new man, but she believed that the apology was genuine.

"I'm glad you came to see me, too," she said.

Richard leaned forward and took his daughter's hands in his own. "Forget the grocery shopping," he started. She'd already forgotten about it because of everything that had happened. "Let's go out to eat. It'll be my treat. We can get some dinner and spend time together."

She nodded reluctantly. It wasn't what she expected, a dinner with her father after a day like she was having. But it was another opportunity for him to prove that he was different now, interested in getting to know her better.

Maybe it was the apology that made her take the offer, or maybe it was something else. Either way, April decided to accept the offer. After a few moments of thoughtful silence, she finally said, "Okay, Dad. Let's go out to dinner later tonight."

April was still hesitant and unsure if this was the best idea, but she accepted his offer regardless. She still wasn't sure if he was truly trying to make amends or if this was just another attempt at getting back into her life, but it didn't matter because either way they were spending time together.

She was willing to give it a chance. Maybe this time would be different.

She would have to find out when it was time for dinner.

CHAPTER EIGHTEEN

Sweat dripped from Jackson's brow as he raked through the tall grass. April watched him scrape at the weeds surrounding the fence.

They had already finished cleaning up around the barn by now, all thanks to the hard work of Jackson, the perfect ranch hand. Now, it was time to start spreading out and fixing the overgrown patches of weeds and greenery.

"Do you know who Isaac Greenfield is?" April asked.

Jackson shrugged while not missing a beat with the rake. "Maybe. I think I've heard his name around town recently. What'd he do?"

"He's running for mayor. But he's also the one trying to take down our plans of turning the property into a horse ranch."

Now, Jackson stopped and looked up at her with furrowed brows. "How'd he figure that?"

April explained to Jackson the lengths that Isaac Greenfield had gone in order to get her to back down from her plans of turning the property into a horse ranch. She was furious and felt as if she was being taken advantage of by someone who was short sighted and didn't care about the long term effects his actions could have on the island.

All Isaac wanted was to make her life miserable. He couldn't plow down her property himself, so he was going to make her leave.

She wanted to save the horses not just for her ranch but for their history on the island. They'd been a part of this place as long as anyone could remember.

If Isaac won, he'd be taking the wild horses away from everything they'd ever known. And that infuriated April. She told Jackson all about it with the passion of her fury from the day's events.

Jackson listened intently, nodding every so often. When she finished, he leaned on his rake and shook his head. "Sounds like a piece of work."

April let out a humorless laugh. "You have no idea. He's trying to ruin my life and the lives of the horses on this island."

She looked out into the horizon, her gaze fixated on the endless expanse of greenery. It was the only thing that brought her peace lately, the only thing that kept her grounded amidst all the chaos in her life.

"I just hope that we can win this fight," she said softly.

Jackson began to sift around for the roots of the overgrown plants again. But quietly, he replied, "We will."

April's heart swelled with gratitude. She couldn't believe that she had found someone like Jackson, someone who believed in her cause as much as she did.

It was even more special because he stumbled upon her. She was so unsure of him at first, but he won her over with his expertise. April thought back to the moment he showed up on the property unannounced. Who knew he would become an ally in a fight as big as the one she was in now?

"I appreciate your help in all of this," April said. Jackson simply nodded in response.

He was still a mystery to her. "You said you grew up in Montana? What was that like?" she asked him as she started her own work beside him.

Jackson smiled softly at the question, his eyes glazing over with nostalgia. "It was something else, that's for sure. It was beautiful in its own way. I grew up on a small ranch with my family. We didn't have much, but we made do with what we had. We had a ranch, so I grew up around horses and livestock."

It was small details that she found charming, but still held him in the shadows. "What was your family like?"

"Well, I had one older brother, one younger. We were always getting into some sort of trouble, but we always had each other's backs."

"And your parents?" she asked, trying to dig deeper into him. She wanted to know him more than just the front he put on. This mysterious facade was attractive, but she wanted to hear something, anything about him.

Jackson wiped his sweaty brow as he shrugged. "They were my parents. A mother who worked hard at home raising us, and a father who worked with his hands on the ranch."

April listened intently, fascinated by him. "What kind of animals did you have on the ranch?"

"Mainly horses, but we had a few cattle as well. There were all kinds of little things running around. I used to spend hours just riding horses around the property. So majestic."

She was surprised by his use of the word majestic. It sounded foreign coming out of his mouth, like it didn't quite fit. April liked that he was sharing this new perspective. It was a side of him she hadn't seen yet.

As they worked in silence, April couldn't help but feel drawn to Jackson. There was something about the way he spoke of his past that made her heart flutter. She wanted to know more about him, to peel away the layers of his mysterious exterior.

"Why did you ever leave Montana?" she asked, breaking the silence.

"I knew I'd end up on a ranch again somewhere, but I wasn't sure where. I just wanted to get out of there. My brothers stayed to take care of the farm. I wanted to spread my own wings. I needed to explore before I ever settled down. And well... I ended up never settling down."

As they worked side by side, April snuck a look at Jackson. There was something about him that made her heart race and her cheeks flush. She knew she shouldn't be thinking like this, especially with everything going on, but she couldn't help herself.

"So, what about you, April? What was your childhood like?" Jackson asked, breaking her from her thoughts.

April hesitated for a moment, not sure if she wanted to delve into her past. But something about Jackson made her feel safe.

"I grew up in the city mainly, but we'd come out here for vacations. My parents weren't very happy, and they divorced when I was a teen. I'm an only child, so it wasn't very exciting," she replied, feeling like her story was much less interesting than his.

Jackson looked at her with a sympathetic smile. "I'm sorry to hear that. It sounds like that was tough."

"Thanks," she replied with a smile. She was used to people pitying her, but Jackson seemed to see the strength in her.

As they continued to work, April couldn't help but steal glances at Jackson.

It was hard not to with his large muscles.

Though April was still hung up on Nigel, she felt attracted to Jackson. For a moment, she wondered if she should just let Nigel get back together with Lily. They were clearly still working some things out.

Lily was clearly still interested in Nigel. And she had no clue what he was thinking lately, except that 'it wasn't what it seemed'. Which April didn't believe for a single second.

She was angry with him for sure, but she did like him and was disappointed with how things were going. Being around Jackson felt easy, easier than being around Nigel lately. That seemed to always end in an absolute mess.

But here she was, surrounded by the whistling trees and green pastures where she could really relax. She could stare at Jackson and feel calm. It was different, new. It was something she wanted to consider.

"What other kinds of animals do you think you'll have on the ranch?" Jackson asked out of the blue.

She put a finger on her chin in thought. "Honestly, I haven't given it much thought. I mean, I know I want horses, but I haven't really considered other animals. At least none specifically."

"Well, you should consider getting some cattle. They're kind creatures. And they really provide some great options. A pet, a dairy cow, whatever you want," he explained. "And chickens are always a good option. Eggs could give you more sustainability."

She raised her brows. Jackson really knew his stuff. There was so much to think about, so much to do.

April had stopped herself from getting too far ahead in the planning, for so many reasons including Isaac Greenfield. But it felt nice to dream again.

She smiled at Jackson, feeling grateful for his suggestion. "Thanks for the advice. I'll definitely keep that in mind."

Lately, everything felt uncertain, but April had always been a planner. "Do you think if I got too many animals here, people would be crowding, making it some sort of petting zoo?" she asked him with a smile.

Though she wanted everyone to feel welcome here, she didn't imagine it becoming a tourist attraction. It was supposed to be for the horses, for rehabilitation and therapy for child riders. Her vision for this place didn't include everyone crowding her property just so they could pet a cow.

"I guess I didn't think of that," he explained, brows furrowed and deep in thought. "They are pretty intrusive here. Everyone knows everything. You'd have to keep the special animals in private I guess. Though, I don't think people would crowd for chickens."

"So you're saying I could get away with a flock of chickens, but not an adorable cow?" April asked.

He shrugged. "I guess so. You'd probably have to hide the cow away for save keeping."

April laughed imaging trying to hide a cow from the sight of any onlookers. "A secret cow? I haven't thought about that before."

Jackson chuckled. "Well, every ranch needs a little mystery, right? Keeps things interesting."

April smiled, feeling her heart skip a beat. She couldn't believe how natural it was to talk to Jackson. It was like they had known each other for years, when in reality they had only just met.

She felt grateful to have Jackson here with her, helping her plan and dream. It was a nice distraction from everything else going on in her life.

Including Nigel, who seemed to keep popping into her mind as she felt more and more connected to the mysterious man in front of her. She still didn't know everything about Jackson, but it was nice to know him even a little bit more than she did before.

It made her feel attracted to him. She couldn't help how she felt. And he wasn't doing anything to stop her from getting to know him.

Would he ever have an ex-girlfriend come into town and then not talk to her about it? Maybe. She'd have to get to know him better before she could say for sure.

Until then, she was stuck trying to decipher both Jackson and Nigel.

April took a deep breath and tried to forget all of her thoughts. She needed to relax. As silence fell between her and Jackson, she was able to focus on the nature around her.

She looked out into her fields filled with lush green meadows that stretched to the horizon, blanketed with wildflowers and restless native plants. The area was painted in breathtaking colors of lush greens, dark browns, and bright yellows.

A clear blue sky loomed above with only an occasional fluffy cloud drifting by, a brilliant yellow sun setting over the horizon in the distance.

A fragrant blend of grass clippings, soil, and sweet flowers mingled with an earthy aroma that made her feel as though she stepped into a lush paradise. The gentle buzz of crickets, the chirping of birds, and the whirring of grasshoppers in the fields filled the air with a peaceful melody.

April took it all in, tearing up at the beauty it showed her. The sound of a gentle breeze rustled through the trees and long grass, singing a song of tranquility.

She couldn't imagine being anywhere else. It was absolutely perfect.

Soon, she would have to return to the chaos of her life. Nigel, her father, Isaac, the money she didn't have in her bank account.

But for now, she had this. And all that mattered was that she was going to fight for this peace until she was sure it would be safe.

CHAPTER NINETEEN

April stared at the email, feeling her stomach twist and turn. It was a lot of money. More than she had anticipated. The peace from working outside quickly wore off as soon as she stepped back into the hotel and opened her laptop.

The University website stated all of Georgia's tuition laid out by category. The math made sense, but April still didn't like the number.

She sighed, feeling the weight of the expenses she was about to face. She had to find a way to come up with the money. It wasn't something Georgia should be worrying about. She had enough on her plate with her studies.

She needed to find a way to make ends meet. The renovations were expensive, and the bed and breakfast wasn't ready to be bringing in tons of profit for her individually.

Her savings were dwindling more by the day. And she couldn't just magically come up with thousands of dollars. Her mind raced with possible solutions, but none seemed viable. She couldn't simply ignore the cost, but she couldn't come up with the money on her own either.

April knew it was time. She had to call her ex-husband, Carl. There had to be a time for him to take some part in this. Now was his chance.

The phone rang four times before he picked up. The phone erupted with noise which took over even as Carl tried to yell into his end of the call, "Hello?"

"Carl? What's going on?"

His mumbles were hardly intelligible. April couldn't tell if it was because he was quiet or everything else was so loud. "I can't hear you!" she yelled back into the phone, frustrated.

"Sorry, sorry. Give me a minute."

April waited impatiently while Carl tried to find a quieter spot to talk. As she waited, she couldn't help but wonder why she was even bothering with him. He had left her high and dry, and now she was calling him to help their daughter out.

The daughter that he left behind while he went off and had his own midlife crisis. But she didn't have any other options. She had to try.

Finally, Carl's voice came back on the line, out of breath, but much clearer now. "Hey, sorry about that. What's up?"

April took a deep breath, trying to keep her composure. "No, everything is not okay. I got the bill for Georgia's tuition, and it's a lot more than I expected. I can't afford it on my own."

"I see," he replied. "How short will you be?"

"Thousands," she replied. It was the truth. The money in savings was for emergencies, among so many other things. She'd budgeted for Georgia, but the tuition had been raised more than four thousand dollars. That wasn't something she could rearrange in her little budget.

There was a long silence on the other end of the line. April wasn't sure he was even still there. "Are you able to help out at all?"

The silence on the other end should have been enough to give April her answer, but she didn't give up hope yet. She waited anxiously for any kind of response.

"Uh, I can barely afford my own living situation right now, actually." She couldn't believe he'd run out of money. After taking what she had in the bank accounts, he still spent it all like a kid in a candy shop. He was even more reckless than when they were married.

When he said he wanted to tour the circuses of the world, April thought he was crazy. But she didn't realize that he would be so careless as to spend every penny on seeing clowns and gymnasts.

April felt a wave of anger wash over her. This was typical of Carl. Always running away from his responsibilities and leaving her to pick up the pieces. She couldn't believe she'd even thought he might help.

"What happened? How are you out of money already?" She rolled her eyes, glad that her ex-husband couldn't see her full annoyance. It would only end in more of a fight than this was going to be.

Carl let out a long sigh. "Look, I've been going through a rough patch. I didn't plan on spending so much on the tour. But I've got a job. That's why it was so loud."

Everything ended in a rough patch with him. Of course he wasn't prepared for an expense like this, that he knew would come. He always relied on April to make sure things were okay.

"What job are you working now?"

Carl paused. "I'm beekeeping in Ghana. I found a nice farm and they're showing me how to keep them."

She had to physically fold in half to stop the laughter from rolling out of her. Of course, he was off doing something crazy. She wondered if it was really the only or best job he could find. There were so many other jobs there that he would probably be more qualified for.

April imagined him going through the list of job posts on his phone and finding the one that sounded the most interesting at the time. He probably arrived and found out how much work it really was and hated it.

He sounded miserable, and she wasn't ashamed to say it made her a little bit happy to hear.

But this call wasn't for her, it was for their daughter who needed them. Quickly, April pulled it together and tried to continue the conversation.

"Listen, I understand that you're having a tough time, but I need your help. Georgia needs your help," she said, trying to keep her voice calm.

"It's not like I'm leaving her high and dry," Carl snapped back. "I just can't help out financially right now. Give me a little while, and I'll figure something out."

Like she believed that would ever actually happen. It would be years before he would probably get back to her. She knew she would have to figure this out on her own. It was ridiculous, but she was used to it by now. She should have known that Carl was going to be no help.

It made her happy to know that at least he was miserable somewhere out in his travels. He'd made her miserable for so long, it was finally his turn to face the consequences of his actions.

April took a deep breath and tried to keep her emotions in check. She couldn't let Carl's behavior ruin her daughter's future. "Fine. I'll figure it out on my own," she said, her voice steady.

"Thanks, April. I really appreciate it," Carl said, sounding relieved.

"Don't thank me yet," April muttered, hanging up the phone before he could say anything else.

She sat there for a few minutes, trying to come up with a plan.

As she walked to the room she had to clean for the guest arriving, she had trouble thinking anything at all. It was like the gears inside of her head weren't spinning. It was full of spider webs, exhausted from the day's troubles.

The room she had to turn over was full of trash from an older single man. It took her minutes to clean everything from the ground and tables.

As April cleaned, she couldn't help but think about how unfair it was that she had to do everything on her own. She had always been the responsible one, the one who made sure everything was taken care of. And now, she had to figure out how to support her daughter all by herself.

April knew it wouldn't be easy, but she was determined to do whatever it took to provide for her daughter. She couldn't let Georgia suffer because of her father's irresponsibility.

The cleaner she sprayed on the wood smelled strongly of lemons. She made her way to the bathroom, where she would spend the most time scrubbing. As she began to use a sponge on the counter, she noticed something she hadn't when she was cleaning out the trash.

Something else had gone missing. The space beside the sink wasn't always so empty. It once held a gold soap dispenser. Obviously it wasn't pure gold, but it shined and gave the white counters a pop of color.

It was another one of her favorite pieces, even though this one they just picked up from the local department store and not from the antique shop.

April felt a pang of anger and frustration rise within her. How could someone just steal a soap dispenser? It seemed like such a small thing, but it was just another added stressor to her already chaotic life.

Whoever was stealing was really beginning to bother her. It wasn't a coincidence anymore. Not just a single object taken by a guest. This was something else entirely.

She had worked hard to create a comfortable and welcoming environment for her guests, and it hurt to know that someone had taken advantage of that.

It had definitely been here before the last guests arrived. She knew because she had filled it up herself when Millie asked where the soap was kept.

In that case, it either had to be the last guest that was here or who she had suspected earlier when something from her own room went missing. It had to be her father.

April's mind was flooded with anger. How could he do this to her? She had already been struggling to make ends meet, and now he was taking things from her own home. It was a violation of her trust and her space.

It was hard to imagine that anyone else could be responsible. He was the only one connected to them all. And he was here all day, with access to her room.

She finished cleaning the bathroom, trying to push the anger and frustration to the back of her mind. But it loomed in the back of her mind.

Her father had been stealing from her. After everything she was doing for him. She was more than frustrated.

All of her anger was taken out as she scrubbed the bathroom floors. She put her bad energy into the sponge and hoped it wouldn't come back again.

As she finished up her cleaning, she left the room, proud that it was spotless. The lobby was nearly empty, but she heard guests shuffling and mingling in the kitchen. Which reminded her of how hungry she was.

That's when she saw him. Her father, walking out of his room and straight up to her.

How could she trust him after knowing that he was probably stealing her things? She was furious, confused. Was it really him doing this to her after all they'd been through?

Could he be the one stealing her precious items that she spent so long picking out?

April's eyes narrowed as she looked at him, trying to find any hint of guilt on his face. But he just smiled at her, a fake and overly sweet smile that made her blood boil.

April tensed up as her father approached her, her fists clenching at her sides. Whatever was happening in her bed and breakfast, she wanted to know. And she wanted answers, now.

Richard's smile spread across his face. "Hey, hun. Are you ready for dinner?"

CHAPTER TWENTY

As they walked into the nice restaurant her father picked out, April was taken aback by the atmosphere of the place. The walls were a deep red color and were adorned with golden frames that held paintings of different styles. The tables were all covered in white tablecloths, and each one had a small vase filled with pink roses.

It was an upscale restaurant with dim lighting and subtle music playing in the background.

She took a deep breath as they walked deeper inside and made their way to a table near one of the windows. The smell of delicious food filled her nose as she settled into her seat across from her father.

April was impressed by the inviting atmosphere that seemed to embrace them both.

The waiter had already taken their orders and left them alone to talk.

The tension between them was palpable as they both sat quietly, neither one wanting to be the first one to start talking. Finally, Richard broke the silence.

"Thanks for coming out with me tonight."

April nodded. "Of course. I'm glad we could find time to get together."

She wasn't sure how she felt about him, but she was glad it was time spent with him like she'd promised. Her father had given her a hard time since the moment he arrived.

And then there was this whole stealing problem.

Richard cleared his throat. "Listen, April. I know I've been difficult the past few days, but I want you to know that I'm thankful for what you've done for me. For letting me stay at the house and spend time with you. I appreciate it."

Her father's words hit a soft spot. It confused her more than anything because she didn't realize how self-aware he truly was.

"Thanks, dad," she replied, unsure of what to say. It had been a hard few days, but she was glad she'd decided to give him a chance. At least then, she would know she tried her best.

How could she ever turn away her own father?

The waiter came back with the food and placed it in front of them. April's eyes widened as she looked at the plate before her. The steak was cooked to perfection and served with a side of mashed potatoes and steamed vegetables.

Then she glanced around the restaurant, taking in all of its beauty.

April looked up to her father, wondering if he could actually afford this restaurant. She hadn't seen him work since he'd arrived, so she couldn't be sure where his money was coming from or where he had gotten enough money to pay for such an extravagant meal.

Richard hadn't paid her a penny since staying with her. She covered everything, the groceries, the house bills, all on her own. What money did he have to be throwing at steak and potatoes?

Her suspicions grew stronger as she watched her father take a bite of his steak. She wondered if he had been stealing from her to pay for such a luxurious meal. But she couldn't quite bring herself to confront him just yet.

"Have you ever been to South America?" he asked her as he bit another piece of juicy steak off of his fork.

She could barely focus on his words as her thoughts were elsewhere. "What? Uh... I don't think so."

"Well, I did a few years back. It was an amazing experience. The scenery is like nothing you've ever seen before. The jungles and the beaches, the mountains and the rainforests, it's all so beautiful."

She wasn't sure why her father was telling her this. It wasn't like she could leave everything and vacation like he did constantly.

He continued taking bites of his steak as he told his story. "We visited these ancient ruins one time. It was just my buddy and I and this tour guide. There was some creepy stuff going on. Apparently we stood right where a slaughter took place."

April looked down at her plate covered in sauce that suddenly looked less appetizing. Still, she tried to pay attention to her father's words. They were supposed to be bonding. This was what he came for.

"And then we rode down the river into these hidden coves. We actually got to swim in them. It was pretty cool."

He looked up with a smile that slowly faded as he realized April wasn't as interested. "Oh, sorry," she said immediately. "I'm listening. I'm just taking it in. South America sounds like a lot of fun."

"It was. I think you should go sometime," he said, regaining the excitement he had.

April nodded, trying to ignore the growing suspicions in her mind. "Maybe I will someday."

She couldn't help but feel like her father was trying to distract her from the real issue at hand. The fact that he had been stealing from her was still gnawing at her, and she knew she had to confront him eventually.

Still, she wondered if this was the right time to bring all of that up. They were supposed to be having a nice dinner. It was their chance to reconnect and start over.

"I saw somewhere that you and Alex went to Wyoming. How was that?" April asked.

Alex was one of her father's best friends. He'd seen more of her father than she had in her entire life.

Richard smiled, happy to change the subject. "Oh, it was incredible. The hiking trails were breathtaking. We even saw a few moose. It was nice to get away from everything for a while."

April wondered what Richard would have to get away from. He had next to no responsibilities. What could his trips possibly help him escape? He didn't have anything to run from.

She put on her best smile, trying to be happy to hear her father talk about something he enjoyed. She took a bite of her steak, savoring the flavor.

"That's great, dad." April nodded, feeling a pang of jealousy. She wished she could have gone on a vacation instead of being stuck at home, worrying about her crazy life.

But then something caught her eye. A flash of silver in her father's jacket pocket. She tried to play it cool, but her heart was pounding in her chest. Was it something else he'd stolen from the bed and breakfast?

As Richard continued to talk about his adventures, April's mind was racing with thoughts of what could be in that pocket. She tried to focus on the conversation at hand, but her eyes kept darting back to that glimmering silver.

Finally, she couldn't take it anymore. "Dad, what's in your pocket?" she blurted out. She couldn't shake the feeling of unease that was creeping up on her.

Richard's eyes widened, caught off guard by her sudden question. "What? Oh, it's just a little something I picked up on my travels," he said, trying to brush it off.

April wasn't satisfied with his answer. "Can I see it?" she asked, her voice firm.

"Of course," he said, slowly pulling the silver pocket watch from his pocket.

As she examined it more closely, she realized it was nothing she recognized. It gave her a breath of fresh air.

"It's lovely," she said with a smile. "Which travel brought it to you?"

Richard hesitated for a moment before answering. "Oh, this one was from my trip to Europe last year. I found it in an antique shop in Paris."

April's suspicions eased a little at his answer. She handed the watch back to him and tried to focus on the rest of their dinner, but her mind was still racing with questions.

Did this mean that he wasn't a thief, or that he just didn't steal the pocket watch?

She couldn't help but feel like there was more to the story. But for now, she decided to let it go. She needed to investigate further, but was this really the right time? When they were finally able to bond?

As her father continued to talk about his recent adventures, her throat grew incredibly dry. She began to overthink everything that happened the past few days. The jewelry box, the elephant, the gold soap dispenser.

The secret that she knew he was probably stealing from her sat like a rock in her stomach.

In every instance, Richard was nearby. He had a history of coming back just to take things from her and her mother. Usually it wasn't objects, it was time, money, love. Things that he wouldn't return.

Now she was convinced that it was him. His pocket watch was just a fluke. Her paranoia is looking for a reason to confront him now. Which she should be doing instead of pretending like everything is fine.

When the waiter brought the check, April tensed up. She hadn't seen how much it cost and she hoped that Richard had enough money to cover it. Her suspicions began to return as he took out a wad of cash and laid it on the table with a flourish.

He clearly had more money than what she was used to seeing him have, and it made her question again where he'd gotten all this cash from.

The probability that he took her things and sold them for the cash was so high. It was all she could think about until she couldn't have convinced herself of any other possibility.

"Dad, can I ask you something real? Like serious," she said, cautiously.

"Of course," he replied with a smile.

April swallowed hard. "Did you take those things from the bed and breakfast?"

"What?" His brows furrowed, and he sat up straighter in his chair. "What things?"

"There's been little... trinkets going missing. I think you took them. An elephant, a soap dispenser, little items have disappeared."

Her father stared at her in disbelief. His mouth dropped open as he thought about his words carefully. It made April's nerves even worse. She was terrified about what he would say next.

"I can't believe you think I would steal from you. What have I done to make you think I would ever do something like that?"

April didn't want to mention the fact that he'd left her several times before, even throughout her childhood. But that wasn't what this was really about. It was about stopping him from taking everything else in the bed and breakfast she'd worked so hard for.

"I mean, you did just pay for dinner with a wad of cash. This is a nice place. How can you afford to go here? You don't have a job or any income," she tried to explain kindly, though it didn't work. It was hard to say 'get a job and stop stealing from me' nicely.

Richard's face hardened. "I have my ways," he said cryptically. "But I assure you, I am not stealing from you or anyone else. I may not have a traditional job, but I have my own sources of income."

April didn't know what to believe. She wanted to trust her father, but the evidence seemed to be against him. Her heart sank. She had been hoping for some sort of explanation, but his reaction only confirmed her suspicions. A mix of anger and disappointment washed over her.

"I just need to know if you took the things from the house. Please, I need the truth," she said, her voice shaking with emotion.

Richard shook his head. "I haven't taken anything from you, April. You're jumping to conclusions. I can't believe you would do this to me."

Before April could jump in, he continued, his voice raising little by little, "And I don't appreciate your accusations. This is getting ridiculous."

"Dad, wait," she said, reaching a hand across the table to grab his. Before she could, her father stood and grabbed his things, storming off towards the door.

April felt like she'd been punched in the stomach. She had wanted to believe her father so badly, but this was all too much for her. Tears welled up in her eyes as she watched him walk away, and she felt horrible for confronting him like that.

She had confronted her father with her suspicions, and it had only made things worse. She wanted to apologize, but she knew it was too late.

Sitting there alone, April felt a mix of guilt and sadness. Clearly, she had upset her father. She shouldn't have confronted him, especially in such a public place.

She thought about that as she walked home. Richard was already gone by the time she started down the street. Thankful she wasn't going to run into him, she realized she had time to think on her own.

The more she thought, the more April started to realize that maybe her father wasn't the one who was stealing all along. Sure, he had money and didn't have a job to explain where it came from. But there were other possibilities.

Maybe he was doing odd jobs for people? Or perhaps he had received an inheritance from a relative? It could be anything, really.

She knew her dad wasn't perfect, but she also knew deep down that he wouldn't do something like this to her. He may not have been the best father in the world, but he wouldn't steal from her.

When she could see the house in the distance, she realized that if her father wasn't stealing from her, that meant someone else was.

Who could want all of her knickknacks? Why would someone want to take her things?

It was a question that demanded answers. She would find those answers, just not today.

CHAPTER TWENTY ONE

The next morning, April awoke to an empty bed and breakfast. There were no guests scheduled for the entire day and evening. The house was still and quiet, with all of her things exactly as she had left them the night before.

In fact, the house was a little too quiet. Not another sound came from outside of her room. April walked the main floor, looking in each part of the lobby, kitchen and entryway. Her father was nowhere to be found.

At first, she thought it was strange that her father hadn't returned home yet, until she noticed that his bedroom door was slightly ajar. It was then that April realized he must have gone somewhere else for the night.

There was an eerie silence that filled the air. But it was welcome compared to the chaos of the day before.

Because there were no guests to attend to, Millie had no reason to come in and work. She had the day off, the first in the past three consecutive days. April guessed it was a welcome break, just as it was for her.

As April wandered the empty house, she couldn't shake the feeling that something was off. It was as if the entire place was holding its breath, waiting for something to happen.

She decided to take advantage of the peace and quiet by doing some much-needed renovations on the bathroom she recently tiled.

It was the only productive thing she felt like she could check off her list for the day.

April rolled up her sleeves and got to work. She carefully removed the old grout from the tub. She worked methodically, losing herself in the task at hand. It was therapeutic, almost zen-like.

She moved to the sink and began to remove the grout from around the tall structure. It was tough at first, her hands growing tired of the repetitive motions, but she got the hang of it after a few frustrating breaks.

As she worked, she thought about her father. Where could he have gone? Was he avoiding her after their argument? Or was he out trying to prove his innocence?

April pushed those thoughts aside and focused on the task at hand. She had to get as much done as she could while no one was there. It felt good to know that she could make as much noise as she needed to.

As April finished up the grout, she carefully hammered around the base of the sink, preparing it to come out. She had a beautiful vanity ready to go in.

If she was being honest with herself, she was growing impatient. She wanted it to go in as soon as possible so she didn't have to worry about the room any longer.

Carefully, she began to tug at the heavy sink. For a moment, she wondered if she should call someone to help her. But then she thought about how she was a strong and independent woman. She wanted to do things on her own.

It reminded her of not too long ago when Georgia was helping her make the house into something of their dreams. They did a ton of the work by themselves. April was proud of that.

So she hunkered down and pulled at the heavy heap of stone, tugging at the sink until it slowly came free. She had to work it back and forth until it began to move forward.

Finally, she got it away from the wall. "Yes!" she yelled, struggling to regain her breath.

April sat on the edge of the tub, satisfied with her work. That was until she felt her feet begin to get wet. Her shoes were filling with water. The bathroom was filling with water.

In a rush of panic, April flew down the stairs and then into the basement. It took her a minute to remember exactly where the water shut off valve was, but eventually she found it.

Breathless, she leaned against the wall of the basement. What had she done wrong?

As she caught her breath, April headed back upstairs to figure out what went wrong.

While she was examining the area behind the sink, she realized that the water damage came from a broken pipe. It was a small crack in the copper that had been severely rusted. She cursed under her breath, angry that she had missed it during her inspection.

The reason the rust had cracked was from when she pulled out the sink. It scraped against the piping and clawed it open.

100

Now she stood in a pool of water that leaked slightly out onto the wooden floors of the adjoining bedroom.

She couldn't believe it. All the hard work she had put into the room was gone in a matter of seconds.

Her mind raced with the thought of how much it would cost to fix. She couldn't afford to pay a plumber, not with everything else she had going on.

But she couldn't just leave it unfixed. The water would ruin the floors and walls and possibly damage the foundation of the house. She had to turn the water back on eventually for the incoming guests.

To start, she began moping up the floor with large towels.

But as she worked, she couldn't shake the feeling of defeat and frustration. It seemed like every time she tried to make progress in her life, something else went wrong and set her back even further.

April shook her head, pushing those thoughts aside. She couldn't afford to dwell on the negative. She needed to focus on finding a solution to the problem at hand.

The floor was finally dry, and April sat on her phone researching ways to cut off the plumbing to the sink. The only viable solution that included tools she already has was to block off the water supply down the line.

It took her a minute to find, but eventually she figured out where the next shut off was and turned it until it closed.

Just as she was about to sit on the floor and wallow in her frustrations, a knock came to her door.

A young man in jeans and a black sweatshirt was standing outside. In the distance, she could hear the hum of a large engine.

She peeked out of the window before opening the front doors to the entryway. Some kind of mail truck sat outside. Not the typical Sandcrest one, but one from a delivery company.

Cautiously, she opened the door. "How can I help you?" she asked, looking through the sliver of the opening she put in the doorway.

"April Faith? I have a special envelope for you. I need a signature," he said in a husky voice.

"Oh, alright," she said, opening the door wider.

As she signed the paper on the clipboard he handed over, April asked, "Who is it from?"

"I just deliver it. I don't know," he replied in a monotone and rehearsed tone, as if he'd been asked a hundred times already.

April nodded and took the envelope from him. She closed the door, feeling a sense of curiosity and excitement wash over her. She had never received a package like this before.

She tore the envelope open and pulled out a letter, her eyes skimming over the words as she read.

As she reached the end, she felt a knot form in her stomach.

Please be advised that your property is on watch by the city council due to a new regulation that will be put into law tomorrow, the sixteenth.

New regulation 12.367 in section B states that no homeowners will be allowed to house any animals, even those referred to as pets, on the island that can be at any time referred to as livestock or pack animals.

Her heart sank in her chest. Was this truly happening? Isaac had found a way to bother her even further by making it law that she couldn't ever have horses in her ranch?

It was just another way to push her to her limits. He wanted to irritate her and it was working, almost too well. Of course, this would make her miserable. He knew that this was her dream, no matter how many times she tried to convince the town otherwise.

And what was the beginning of the letter? Some kind of warning that they were watching her? It had to be considered a threat. April wasn't sure what else she could call it.

Isaac wanted her to know that he would be watching very carefully for the one moment she stepped out of line.

She had to be more careful than ever, which made her anxious. Her heart raced in her chest.

April took a deep breath and tried to calm herself down. She couldn't let Isaac's petty actions get the best of her. She had worked too hard to let him ruin everything she had built.

She took a deep breath and forced herself to calm down. But less than a second later, her phone buzzed in her pocket. The paper crinkled in her hands as she jumped at the noise.

"Oh, gosh," April exclaimed aloud. "It's just a phone, April. Try to relax."

Rolling her eyes at herself, she pulled out her phone and pressed answer. "Hello, this is April Faith."

"Hi, April," a familiar voice responded. "It's the Millers, we stayed at your property just this past week."

It was the woman from the adorable couple who'd stayed. They were so kind to her throughout their stay. And then she wondered for a while if they were the ones who stole from her. Of course, that was quickly washed away when she suspected her father.

"Of course! What can I help you with? I hope you didn't have any trouble."

"No, no, definitely no trouble. But we did notice that I'm missing my favorite pair of earrings. They were these little pearls that I'd set out on the nightstand." She sighed on the other end of the line. "He thinks I've misplaced them, but I specifically remember setting them in my bag on the nightstand during our stay."

"Oh, no," April replied. "I'm sorry. I haven't seen them, but if you give me just one moment, I can go check the room for you."

"Sure," the woman said before April put the call on mute and set the phone down on the desk.

April quickly walked back to the room they stayed in. She searched high and low for the pair of earrings, but turned up with nothing. She thought she would have seen the pair of nice earrings before. After all, she'd done a thorough search for her jewelry box when it ended up missing from the same room.

When she got back downstairs, she was slightly winded from turning the room upside down. "Yeah, I'm sorry, but I didn't find anything. Are you sure it didn't get lost in that bag? Or maybe you just misplaced it and it's somewhere else?"

"No, I've emptied the bag completely. All of our bags, in fact." The woman sounded disappointed, rightfully so. April felt horrible for her. She knew what it felt like to have things go missing. "And I specifically remember putting them in the bag."

April now looked around the desk. Maybe someone had turned them in, and Millie hadn't told her yet. "I'm sure we'll find them. They have to be somewhere," she tried reassuring the woman.

"Maybe your helper saw it? She said she was going to restock our room the day before we left. Could you ask her if she happened to see it anywhere? That might be able to tell us when it went missing."

And April put all the pieces together. She never asked Millie to check on guests in the middle of their stay. They had been stocking the rooms with enough that the guests wouldn't need anything else while there.

That way they wouldn't have to continue to entering and housekeeping while they were trying to enjoy their trip.

The only reason Millie could have been in that room was to take Mrs. Millers' earrings. The jewelry box that sat on the dresser was just another casualty, something else she took for herself.

But she couldn't let the couple know what had happened. Not until she knew that Millie had the pearl earrings.

And it would look incredibly unprofessional if it became known that she hired someone who stole from people. Her credibility would go down the drain.

"I'll try talking to her. In the meantime, I'll keep an eye out for them and call you if we find anything," April said, reassuring her.

"Thank you so much, April. We really appreciate it," Mrs. Miller replied before hanging up.

April put her head into her hands. What else could possibly go wrong?

CHAPTER TWENTY TWO

April sat on the floor in the lobby of her bed and breakfast, feeling defeated. She thought about how not much else could go wrong at this point. It felt like a never-ending cycle of bad luck.

She was so exhausted that all she wanted to do was curl up into a ball and sleep until it all went away.

Her mind wandered to the past few days and all of the events that had taken place. It felt like her world had been turned upside down.

April thought back to all the other guests who had stayed at her bed and breakfast over the past few days. What else had occurred that hadn't been reported yet?

Did her father start arguments with any of them? Had Millie stolen from anyone else?

What she saw was only the surface. Just like with Isaac. Who knew what else he had planned for her?

After taking a moment to herself to reflect, she got up and went to the kitchen to make herself a cup of coffee. As she opened the cupboard, she noticed that the jar of coffee beans was almost empty. Great, just another thing to add to the list of things she needed to take care of.

She grabbed her phone and opened up the notes app. She added "buy coffee beans" to the list of things she needed to do.

As she stared at the phone in her hand, a call flashed across the screen. It was an unknown number, which made her nervous. She bit her bottom lip as she answered.

"Hello?"

An unwelcome familiar voice came through the line, "Hey, April."

It was Maxwell, her boss from the law firm. After finding her at the house months ago, he decided to hit on her and then beg her to come back to the office. There was nothing more he could say.

"What do you want?" she replied angrily. April knew she should have just hung up, but she couldn't help being curious in what he had to say for himself.

"The firm has been struggling," he said through gritted teeth. She could tell that this was the last thing he wanted to do. It was clearly his last resort. "We would like to offer you a position back on the team."

April rolled her eyes and leaned against her counter. "You already did that. I turned you down, or do you not remember?"

She hoped the words hit him, and he thought about what he did to her. If he was a good boss, he wouldn't hit on his employees. He was a jerk. And she would never forget that.

"We have a different offer to send you. I wanted to let you know before it came up in your inbox so you know it's real. April, it's a fifty percent increase."

April was taken aback. She hadn't expected this. She knew she could use the extra money to help take care of the bed and breakfast. And it was a lot of money.

She thought that she was done with her career in the legal field. Why were they offering her such a good deal? "What's in it for you?" she asked, knowing that deals like this never came without strings.

"We get you back," he replied quietly.

It was blatantly obvious that Maxwell wasn't the one who wanted her back. It was the board and senior members who forced him to talk to her.

Usually, she wouldn't even consider it. But with everything going on, she didn't want to turn it down right away. April suspected she would say no, but there was too much to think about to make a decision right away.

"I'll consider your offer," she replied plainly. "Have a good day, Maxwell."

"Thank you," he said before hanging up.

He hadn't gained any charm since she left. In fact, she could tell that he'd gotten even grumpier than when she was there.

April walked over to the couch and sat down. She held her phone tightly in her hand, wondering if she should take the offer.

On one hand, she could use the extra money. On the other hand, she didn't want to go back to that toxic environment. She loved her life here, the one she was building anyway.

The offer was tempting, but she wasn't sure if she wanted to go back to the law firm. Not after what had happened with Maxwell. It would mean leaving the bed and breakfast, the place where she finally felt like she belonged.

But the thought of having more financial stability was tempting, especially with all the problems going on in her life here.

April sighed and put her phone down. She wasn't sure what to do. She needed to think about it, but she didn't want to stay inside anymore.

Grabbing a light jacket, she stepped out of the door. The air was cool and salty from the ocean.

Careful of her step, she walked down the stairs to her private beach area, looking out over the waves. It was a typical fall day, windy and cloudy.

As soon as April stepped onto the beach, she was overcome by a sense of calm. The sound of the waves crashing against the shore filled her ears and gave her some peace of mind. She walked along the sand, letting the cool ocean breeze blow through her hair.

The waves crashed against the shoreline, creating a soothing sound that filled April's ears as her feet sunk into the sand with each step.

The sun sparkled off the surface of the water. As she looked out over the ocean, she felt just how vast and endless the sea truly was. Seagulls down the shoreline began to squawk.

It was truly one of the most beautiful days she'd seen.

As April continued walking, she felt a sense of clarity wash over her. She closed her eyes and took a deep breath, letting the salty air fill her lungs.

And that's when she heard the distant thunder. Within seconds, water began to fall from the sky. Rain poured down her face onto her shoulders. Her clothes were soaked in minutes of walking back towards the house.

She couldn't even walk outside to get some clarity on her situation. Even the weather didn't want her to win.

The only thing she was thankful for was the fact that the rain washed away her gentle tears.

April rushed inside the house and grabbed a beach towel to dry off. When April was finally dry, she sat on the couch and thought about what would happen if she left all of this behind.

The thought of leaving the bed and breakfast made her heart sink. She had worked so hard to make it a place that felt like home.

But then there was the money. She could use that money to help with some of her financial struggles. It would certainly make life easier for her and those around her.

The thought of leaving her newfound home filled her with a pang of sadness. She had worked so hard to create the life here that she had now.

April knew that this would be a difficult decision. None of it made any sense. Either way, she felt like she was making a mistake.

Suddenly, her phone began to ring. "What now?" she said aloud. But it was Georgia's name that flashed across the screen.

April smiled and answered the call. "Hi honey," she said warmly.

Her daughter's voice sounded so far away, but it was filled with love. "Hey, mom. How's it going?"

"It's fine. What's up? Did something happen?" For a moment, April wondered if Georgia was calling about the tuition. She wasn't ready to come up with the missing few thousand dollars yet.

April knew she would be able to cover it, but it would take some time. She just didn't want Georgia to know that she was struggling. That was something her daughter should never have to worry about.

Georgia chuckled. "Can't a daughter call her mom? Just to talk?"

She felt a wave of relief wash over her as she heard her daughter's laughter through the phone line. She knew that this conversation was exactly what she needed right now.

"Of course you can," April said, smiling. She let out a deep sigh.

After a short pause, Georgia said, "What's wrong, mom?"

"What do you mean?" she tried to say, though she knew her daughter would catch on. It was hard to hide things from her, especially feelings as strong as these ones.

"I can tell something's bothering you, so dish."

Georgia had opened the flood gates and April couldn't hold it all in anymore. She told her about almost everything that was troubling her.

She kept the tuition close to her heart as a guarded secret she hoped Georgia would ever know.

And she decided that talking about Nigel too much wasn't the best idea either. After all, it'd been less than a year since she'd divorced Carl. Georgia needed time to process. She didn't need to hear about the details of her mother's new love life.

But April told her about everything else. Isaac, the villain running for mayor that was trying to take her down. Richard, her father, who was asking for everything under the sun to be perfectly made for him. And Millie, her new hire, who was stealing from everyone at the bed and breakfast.

Then she told her daughter about the job offer she'd just received.

"Maxwell called you? That jerk?"

April nodded even though she knew Georgia couldn't see her. "Yes, I was surprised too," she said.

Georgia scoffed. "I hate that guy. You have to tell him no. Tell me you turned it down."

April was quiet for a moment. She thought about the money and how badly she wanted it to help her family.

But she also thought about how much she had invested in the bed and breakfast and how much she would leave behind if she took this job.

"Well... I didn't tell him no. But I didn't accept the job. I asked for time to consider the offer. It's for way more money. I can't just turn it down right away," April tried to explain.

Georgia let out a sigh. "Mom. You can't. There's no way you're going back to that miserable job with that miserable man."

April didn't know what to say. Stumbling on her words, she replied, "I know. I'm just trying to do the right thing. And this job offer is a lot of money. It could really help us. I just don't want to make the wrong decision."

"Mom, I think you should stay. You worked so hard to create this life here, and it's something special. If you go back to that old job, you'll just end up regretting it. I don't think you should give up on something that's been so important to you," Georgia said.

Silence filled the line. April was taken by how passionate her daughter was. It was so refreshing to talk to someone who cared so much. It reminded April of how much she missed her.

When April didn't respond, Georgia got even more firm, "Mom, you cannot take that job. You're a strong, independent woman. There is nothing you can't do. If you want this bed and breakfast and the horse ranch to work out, you have to fight for it."

April felt a sense of pride and comfort wash over her as she listened to her daughter's words. Georgia had always been strong-willed and determined, and it was clear that those qualities had only grown stronger since leaving home.

Georgia was right. She had worked too hard to give up on her dreams now. And she couldn't let the fear of financial struggles hold her back.

She renovated this house all on her own. It was just like learning to swing a hammer. April needed the tools and might to come up with the solutions.

She couldn't just give up on everything she had worked so hard to build.

"You're right, honey. I won't take the job. I'll stay here and fight for what I believe in," April said, determination filling her voice.

"Good," she replied, matter-of-factly. Then softly, she added, "I'm proud of you, mom."

That's all April needed to push forward. Now she was going to grit her teeth and finish what she started.

CHAPTER TWENTY THREE

All it took for April to get the courage to make it through the challenges she faced was her daughter's voice. She needed the support of someone else who cared.

April realized she wasn't alone in this fight. She had other people who would help her along the way.

With newfound strength, April faced each challenge head-on. She tackled every obstacle with a fire that burned hotter than ever before.

April truly understood the power of having a support system.

No matter how hard things got, she could always turn to someone else for help. She didn't have to do everything on her own.

In order to get through all of her problems, April had to focus on them one at a time. Her first order of business was figuring out what to do with Millie.

April felt a sense of betrayal that cut deep. She had trusted Millie and given her a chance, but she had taken advantage of her kindness. April knew she couldn't just let it slide. She had to confront Millie and let her know that her behavior was unacceptable.

April called Millie into her office and sat her down. "Millie, I have to talk to you about something. I have reason to believe that you've been stealing from me and our guests. Do you have anything to say about that?" April asked, her voice stern and unwavering.

Millie immediately began to shake, her face turning pale. She stammered as she tried to deny the accusation, "No! I would never do something like that. I respect you too much."

April could see her hands trembling and knew that Millie was hiding something. She had caught her culprit for sure.

Unable to meet April's gaze, Millie's hands shook as she crossed them in front of her.

"I just need you to be honest with me. You know that I can't have anything like that happening here. I trusted you, and you went behind my back and stole from me. The least you could do is own up to it." April's voice kept firm.

Millie's face finally fell. "I'm really sorry. I did take those things," she replied softly.

"This is exactly what's going to happen next," April began, tapping her fingers on her desk. "You're going to give back everything you took. Everything. Then you're not going to work here anymore. And I won't press charges."

She looked at April, wide eyed. "You're not going to press charges? Why?"

"Because I'm giving you a chance to find another job for yourself and never do this again. Consider yourself lucky," she said.

It took April a long time to decide that she wasn't going to involve the police. But ultimately the decision came down to whether or not it was worth it.

Sending Millie to jail would have only caused more trouble and stress for April. She wanted to focus on her business and move forward, not sit there doing more and more paperwork. Plus, she believed that everyone deserved a second chance.

That didn't mean that she was going to take that chance on her business. But she could send Millie off to at least try her luck with another job.

"I understand. I'm really sorry, April. I messed up big time," she said, tears welling up in her eyes. Millie left the room, her head hung low. April knew that she had made the right decision, even if it wasn't the easiest one.

After Millie left, April felt a sense of relief wash over her. She had taken care of one of her problems.

Now it was time for a big one. April called her father, listening to it ring three times before he picked up.

"Hey, is there any way you could come into the house?" She still wasn't sure where he was staying, but he needed to feel welcomed back in the house. It was her way of extending an olive branch for her wrong.

After a brief pause, Richard replied, "Sure. I'll come over now, if that's alright."

Before she could respond, the call ended. She took a deep breath. This was going to be the hardest conversation yet.

Her father walked into the room with a smile and took a seat in front of April's desk. She could feel her heartbeat quicken as she prepared for the worst.

"Dad, we have to talk," she said as she sat in her chair. "I want to apologize to you. I shouldn't have jumped to conclusions and thought you were stealing from me."

Richard sat silently, staring at April with a snide look. She continued, "I was just so overwhelmed with everything going on, and I lashed out. But I know now that you would never do something like that to me."

"I accept your apology," her father said, arms crossed in front of him. "You really should have fact-checked before you blamed me for all your problems. I would never steal from you."

She nodded. "I know that now. I should have known that then. You're not a thief." He nodded with a satisfied smirk. April knew she was about to wipe it off his face. "And now I want an apology from you."

"What? For what?" His brows furrowed and he leaned forward, dropping his arms to his side.

"For taking advantage of my hospitality here. Before you left, you used me for everything. Your pillows, your groceries, a place to stay, someone to tell your stories to. I want to be there for you, to be your daughter. But that's not what you were doing, was it?"

April leaned forward and waited for his reply. Richard sat back in his chair, his face growing red with anger. "How dare you accuse me of that? I may have needed your help, but I never took advantage of you," he said defensively.

She remained calm, but firm, just like she practiced. "But you did, Dad. You were constantly asking for things. And telling me how I could do things better without helping at all. Every time you wanted something, you came to me. I want you to understand it from my perspective."

Richard looked down at his hands, clasping them tightly together. "I was going through a rough time, April. You have to understand that."

"And I do. But I wish you would have just talked to me about it instead of going back to your old ways of taking advantage of the kindness given to you. Can you at least admit that you could have been better about that?" she said, her tone begging with him to get it.

Her father looked up at her. For the first time in years, she saw the face of her dad, who truly felt bad for what he did. "I'm sorry," he said. "I didn't realize I was doing those things. I know I'm not perfect, but... I tried."

It meant a lot to hear the words she'd been waiting for. Even the slightest amount of responsibility he took for his actions meant that he was improving. "Thank you, dad," April said, smiling at him. "But this next part is going to be hard."

She took a deep breath. "I need you to leave." Her body tensed, bracing for some kind of emotional impact. Richard was going to have an outburst when he heard that he was being kicked out of the house.

"Seriously?" He looked back and forth as if someone was going to help him. "You're kicking out your old man?"

It was supposed to go smoothly, but April knew now that it wasn't going to happen the way she pictured it. She opened her mouth to explain, but her father interrupted her, "After all that? I just apologized to you."

"I know," she began, holding out a hand. "But, you've taken advantage of me. I'm not just going to sit here while you do that. If you want to spend time with me and make amends, then you can do that while not living in this place I built from the ground up."

Richard scoffed and stood up from his chair. "Fine. I'll leave."

April watched as her father stormed out of the room, slamming the door shut behind him. She let out a deep breath, feeling a weight lifted off her shoulders. It was a difficult conversation, but she knew it was for the best.

She hated that it had to come to this, but she knew it was for the best.

It wasn't going to be the hardest thing she did that day.

CHAPTER TWENTY FOUR

April sat down at her desk and surveyed the room. She had already made a lot of progress on renovating the bed and breakfast, but there was still much to be done. She picked up her pen and began writing out her plan for the rest of the renovations.

It seemed like a daunting task, but she was determined to see it through. She began by making a list of all the materials she would need, then furniture, then any room accessories.

Thankfully, she only had the few remaining rooms to work on. She could figure those out no problem. The real issue was getting it done quickly and quietly while guests stayed in the available rooms.

But April was always up for a challenge but, she was prepared to face it head-on. She knew that the bed and breakfast needed to be perfect to attract more customers. She was willing to put in the work to make that happen.

And that's exactly what it would take, work. Because of her newly decreased budget, she would need to do as much work as she could herself.

She made a list of things she thought she could figure out on her own, and things she definitely couldn't.

As she stood in the bathroom where everything went wrong, a pen in her mouth, deep in thought, a knock came to the door.

"Hey, April," Jackson said from the doorway. "Sorry to bother you, I was just working on the weeding down past the barn and I think you might have a Wisteria. So I'll need to run to the store and get supplies to spray it."

April noticed his eyes trailing from her to the broken pipe back to her. "Thank you for the help. I'll reimburse you if you leave the receipt on the desk."

"Right," he replied, keeping his feet firmly planted in the doorway. Silence filled the room as he stared at the wall.

"Jackson?" She asked, smiling. He broke his focus to look at her, wide-eyed.

When he finally came to, he said, "Sorry. I just... What happened in here?"

"Broke a rusty pipe. Just a day ago there was water all over the floor," she said, trying to be light hearted about the tough situation.

Jackson nodded. "Yeah, I can tell. That drywall right there is going to need to be replaced." He pointed to a portion of the wall that had been scratched up and damaged where the water had flowed out. "And you should probably make sure there's no other rust around the plumbing there. Could be dangerous and leak."

Of course. It was another thing to add to her list. She wrote it down in the column where she would need a professional. It was getting longer every minute. She sighed. It would be expensive, but what else could she do?

"Thank you. That's good to know, I guess," she said as he walked over and investigated the area. "I'll have to have someone come look at it."

"No, I can do that for you," Jackson said like it was no big deal.

"What? Seriously?" Her brows raised.

He shrugged his shoulders and stood. "Of course. I actually spent about a year training under a master carpenter. So I have some experience in the field. I'd be more than willing to take some time and help out."

April was shocked by the offer. She had no idea her ranch had was experienced in renovation. This could be more helpful than she ever imagined.

"Oh my gosh, that would be amazing. Thank you so much. I will definitely be taking you up on that offer!"

"No problem," he said, stepping into the room and looking around. "Wow, you've really done a great job with this place."

"Thanks," April said, feeling a sense of pride in her work. "It's been a lot of work, but it's worth it."

She looked into his dark eyes and felt her heart skip a beat. The tension between them was palpable. It was just like when they worked outside together and couldn't seem to look away from each other.

April's mind started to wander as she thought about the chemistry between them. She couldn't ignore the heat that was building in her body as she looked at Jackson.

She wanted to reach out and touch him, to feel the warmth of his skin and the strength of his embrace. But she held back. She was afraid that if she made a move, it would all be over before it even started.

Jackson seemed to sense her thoughts as he stepped closer and said, "Let me know if there's anything else I can do for you."

His voice was low and husky as he moved in closer. His eyes were locked on hers as he leaned in towards her. They stood only a foot apart.

April's heart was beating so loud, she was sure Jackson could hear it. She could feel the heat emanating from his body and the electricity that seemed to be sparking between them.

"Can I ask you something, and you promise not to find it weird?" April said, her cheeks growing hot out of fear of embarrassment.

"Sure," he replied, listening intently.

She wasn't sure how to word it, so she thought through her phrasing carefully. "Does it feel like maybe... there's something here?"

Jackson's gaze flickered from her eyes to her lips and back again. "Yeah," he exhaled. "I think there might be. I've been trying to ignore it, but I can't seem to stay away from you."

April's heart leapt at his words. It was kind and romantic. But there was so much to consider. Nigel, he was still in the back of her mind. Even though he'd hurt her, she cared about him. Her feelings for him didn't just go away because she'd found something new and beautiful to stare at.

She was glad to finally acknowledge her feelings for him, but it had to be kept at that. Not just for Nigel's sake, for her own.

Jackson was technically her employee. She couldn't be seen hiring people and then dating them. Word around town would spread so fast.

"I think that might cause some issues," she said, still smiling.

He nodded. "I thought about that, too. I get what you mean."

"That we can't... Whatever our feelings, we should probably push it away. You're an employee," she explained. "It would be really unprofessional and I don't want anyone getting the wrong idea."

It was disappointing, but April knew she was doing the right thing. Jackson hung his head low. "I understand."

April took a deep breath, feeling the weight of the moment. "I hope this won't make things awkward between us," she said, hoping to ease the tension.

"No, it won't. I'm glad we could talk about it. It's better to be honest than to pretend it's not there."

It was like a magnetic force, the pull between them undeniable, making their eyes lock together even when they tried to look away. The tension was deafeningly silent, as if it were a looming presence towering over them.

"I hope you're not upset," she said softly.

Jackson shook his head. "No, of course not. I understand where you're coming from. It's just... hard to ignore this kind of connection."

As he looked up at her, he must have realized what he said by the conflict in her eyes. "But of course," he got out quickly, "I'll push it away. I can keep to myself for now."

She didn't like the way he said 'for now', as if a storm was brewing and it was coming to wreck her later.

April felt a lump form in her throat. She knew it was for the best, but it still hurt to see the disappointment in Jackson's eyes. She couldn't help but wonder what could have been if things were different.

"I appreciate your understanding," she said, trying to keep her voice steady. "And I value your work here. You're doing a fantastic job."

Jackson gave her a small smile. "Thank you, April. I'll continue to do my best."

They stood there for a moment longer, the tension between them slowly dissipating.

"I'll finish up the work here and then I'll be on my way," Jackson repeated, finally breaking his eye contact to walk towards the doorway. "Have a good day, April. I'll see you tomorrow."

As he turned to leave the room, April couldn't help but feel a pang of regret. She had wanted to explore the chemistry between them, but she knew it was the right decision to keep things professional.

As she watched him leave, she couldn't shake the feeling that something was about to change between them. She didn't know what it was, but she felt like they were on the edge of something different and new.

April continued making her list of renovations that needed to be completed, except this time she added another column. 'Things to ask Jackson'.

It was nice being able to have another place to go for questions and help. She didn't need to rely solely on herself for knowledge and man power.

And looking at this bathroom, she knew she would need something extra. Anything to help her transform this horrid space into something she could be proud of.

As she made her way out of the bathroom, April couldn't help but notice the way the light hit the tiles just so, illuminating the space in a way that made her feel alive. At least she did something right.

CHAPTER TWENTY FIVE

Feeling strange about her conversation with Jackson, April went into town to talk to Nigel.

She knew that she walked away while he was trying to explain himself, and it wasn't right. At least she could have tried to hear him out. Though she wasn't sure what he could say to make her feel any more comfortable about the situation. It was rude of her to walk away like she did.

April wanted to talk to him, to see him again. She wanted her friend back. One of her first and only friends in the small town of Sandcrest.

As April walked down the busy streets of Sandcrest, she couldn't help but feel alive. She passed by the local coffee shop, the scent of freshly brewed coffee wafting through the air. The place was bustling with locals, chatting and laughing over their cups of joe. It was a welcome sight, a reminder that she wasn't alone in this town.

As she walked towards Giant's, April couldn't help but feel nervous. Would he even want to talk to her after she abruptly walked away from him the other day?

When she finally arrived, it was time to head inside the busy burger joint. A tourist held the door open for her as she walked in. She took a deep breath and walked toward her usual seat on the corner bar stool.

She searched around for Nigel, but couldn't see him anywhere. After a few minutes, April decided to wander the restaurant to see if she could find him.

The bartender was busy getting drinks out to the patrons at the bar top. It was hard to see past the people to the kitchen door, where there was a small window she could usually see into.

On her tiptoes, she looked inside and waited for Nigel to pass by again, like he usually did. But no one was walking around back there.

That's when she heard his voice. It was so quiet at first she doubted herself, but then she realized it really was him. His face was hidden by a divider that separated the bar and a row of booths in the back of the restaurant.

She slowly walked over to it, expecting to take him by surprise. But as she turned the corner, she recognized blonde hair and immediately froze. It was his ex-girlfriend here, yet again. It was Lily.

April felt a jolt of shock run through her body as she watched Nigel and Lily stand together beside the divider. They appeared to be engrossed in conversation, their heads close together as he spoke to her.

She felt a tinge of jealousy, wondering what they could possibly be talking about that was so secretive. What else could they have to say to each other?

Maybe they were back together after all. The thought broke April.

She debated whether or not to interrupt them, to make her presence known. It wasn't long ago that she imagined herself telling Lily exactly how she felt.

Now, she could walk over to them and let them know that she was happy they'd found each other. She would say that she would no longer be between them. If Lily wanted him, she could have him. He could run off with her if he wanted.

Her jealousy was on full display, a fire rising inside of her. But then she stopped as she heard the words that came out of his mouth.

"You have to stop doing this," he said softly. "This coming to my work. It needs to stop."

April's heart raced as she heard Nigel's words. Suddenly, the jealousy and anger that had consumed her moments ago were replaced with confusion and concern.

She took a deep breath and stepped closer to the divider, trying to keep her footsteps quiet. She was trying to hear more of their conversation. Nigel continued speaking, his voice barely above a whisper.

"I can't keep doing this, Lily. You need to move on. I can't be with you anymore."

April's eyes widened in shock as she heard his words. This was not what she had been expecting to hear. She had been so sure that Nigel and Lily were back together.

"I just wanted to talk," Lily said, her voice low and husky. "I miss you."

April rolled her eyes. Of course, she was trying to get him back. She knew that from the moment Lily stepped foot in this town. It didn't matter what she said, it mattered how he responded.

"You have to get out. I mean it. I can't have you showing up like this. I'm not interested in you anymore. Two years ago, you broke off our engagement. And honestly, I'm glad you did."

Putting a hand to her mouth, April stopped herself from gasping out loud. She couldn't believe what she was hearing. She'd found out about his past, but didn't realize how over it he truly was.

As she stood there, frozen in place, she saw Lily reach out to touch Nigel's arm.

He pulled away, his expression hardening. "Stop. I mean it. You broke things off, and we need to keep it that way. I don't want you anymore, can't you get that? We broke up for a reason. It's time to move on."

For the first time, April felt like she saw the whole picture. Nigel had been trying to tell Lily this all along, but she struggled to accept the truth.

Lily had come to town to try and get him back, but he was having none of it. Nigel truly wanted April all along.

The scenario where Nigel was flip flopping between the two of them, it was never real. It was all in her head. She thought that he was trying to choose between her and Lily. But maybe he was just trying to let Lily down easy.

April's heart felt like it was swelling with happiness as she watched Nigel stand firm in his decision. She realized that she had been so focused on her own insecurities and jealousy that she had failed to see the truth. Nigel had chosen her all along.

She had been so worried about losing him to his ex-girlfriend, but now she knew that he had never really been interested in Lily. It was a weight lifted off her shoulders.

Lily's shoulders slumped as she turned to leave. Nigel's words had finally sunk in, and she realized that he wasn't going to change his mind.

April dipped slightly behind the divider so they couldn't see her. Then she heard Lily's voice say, "I just want you to know that I love you."

"I know," Nigel said.

As she walked away, April took a step forward, ready to reveal her presence. But something held her back.

Maybe it was because she didn't want to interrupt Nigel's moment of closure with his ex-girlfriend. Or maybe it was because she felt bad for Lily.

She'd been on that end of the breakup before. Lily would find someone new, someone who was better for her. It wasn't Lily's fault that she still had feelings for Nigel.

April's heart swelled with love and relief as she realized that Nigel had been faithful to her all along. She felt ashamed of her jealousy and anger towards Lily.

After a minute had passed, Lily finally out the front door of the restaurant, April stepped out to reveal herself to Nigel.

His eyes grew wide, his cheeks pink. "Uh, hi. I'm sorry, I wasn't really expecting you," he said, stammering.

She smirked. "I thought I'd stop in to see you. I thought maybe we should talk. I guess I was right."

April watched the realization come across his face. "You heard all of that?"

"Every word," she said with a small smile. "I'm sorry for not trusting you. I was so consumed with my own insecurities that I didn't see the truth. You were always faithful to me."

Nigel reached out to take her hand. "I understand why you were jealous. You don't have to apologize. I should have been more open with you. But I promise you, I only want to be with you."

Her eyes peeked at the strong hands by his side. She couldn't resist the urge to take them in hers. "I believe you," she said softly. "And I only want to be with you too."

"I just want us to be honest with each other from now on. No more secrets, no more hiding things from each other," Nigel said.

April felt the warmth of his breath on her skin. She wrapped her arms around him, holding him close as they stood there in the middle of the restaurant.

"I agree," she whispered into his chest.

Nigel's hands rest firmly on her hips as they hugged close together. "Let's start fresh, okay?"

She couldn't have agreed more. "As long as you keep cooking me dinner, I'll be there."

He chuckled, deep and hearty. "It's a deal."

As they pulled away from the embrace, Nigel's eyes locked onto hers. His hands moved up to cup her face softly, and he leaned in closer. Their lips met in a tender kiss, their passion reignited.

It was as if a tidal wave of passion had been building up inside of her, and now it was crashing over them both. It was gentle but held the force of a thousand waves crashing against the shore.

April felt a rush of emotions, a feeling of safety and warmth, of contentment and desire. She knew that Nigel was the one for her, and she was the one for him.

As their lips parted, April smiled up at him. "I'm so glad we found our way back to each other," she said, her voice barely above a whisper.

Nigel smiled back at her, his eyes shining with love. "Me too. I never want to lose you again."

They held each other close, basking in the moment. For the first time in a long time, April felt truly happy. She knew that there would be challenges and obstacles in their relationship, but she was ready to face them with Nigel by her side.

But it wasn't the last challenge she had to face before she felt comfortable again. There was one more thing she had to do.

As she walked out of Giant's hand-in-hand with Nigel, she felt butterflies flapping their bright wings inside of her. They soon made her sick as she thought about her nemesis.

It was time to take on Isaac Greenfield.

CHAPTER TWENTY SIX

Beth typed so ferociously on her laptop that almost the whole kitchen table was shaking. April was thankful she didn't have guests because they would have been very confused at the sight of four women doing a full-blown investigation in the dining room.

"I haven't found any legislation about the pet/pack animals law they sent the letter about," Alice called out from her end of the wooden table.

April typed it out in her document of clues. It was a full page at this point, full of information regarding Isaac and his lies.

"What about you, Kellie?" April asked, looking over at the dark hair barely peeking out from the tablet in front of her.

She shrugged. "I don't see anything here about needing permits before plans are in place with a contractor or before improvements are made to the land."

April had cases like this down to a science. Her history in law seemed to be coming in more handy than she thought it would.

"Okay, that's good to know. And Alice, there wasn't anything in the papers about that law either, right?" April asked, turning to her friend, who was scrolling through pages on her phone.

She shook her head. "Nothing," Alice replied with a smirk.

"I have something!" Beth called out. "I finally got through all of the neighborhood apps, and I combed through my social media friends lists to ask if anyone else got a letter like yours. Nothing. No one else received a warning about livestock on the property."

April wanted to laugh. Isaac had underestimated her big time. He had no idea who he was fighting against. They were going to make sure her business was safe.

Thankful for her friends, April smiled up at them. They were kindly taking their evening to research a man running for mayor. And they were doing fantastic at it.

After everything he did to her, April wanted to make sure that she could tell him off. This time, she'd be prepared. Her words would win.

"Okay, let's focus on the man himself. What do we know about Greenfield?" April asked, taking charge.

April looked up, eyes wide. "You guys have to look at this."

The other three women gathered around her screen. It was an article written by a local paper stating that one of Isaac's companies was donating to a local flower distributor.

Beth and Kellie gasped.

"What is it?" April asked, looking through the article again to see if she missed something.

April looked up at her friend. "You don't see it? That's Stay Green, the flower distributor in town. It's run by Sanchez."

"You mean like... like councilman Sanchez?" April asked, remembering the man who explained all of the paperwork to her when she first went into town hall.

They all nodded. "Yep. That Sanchez," Kellie said. "That means that they're in cahoots. Because why else would they go along with his insane plans and fake a letter telling you to stop what you're doing? They wanted to scare you, but they're the ones doing something wrong."

"He bought them off. He's trying to pay his way to office and bribe them to get you to stop," Beth explained in plainer language.

She couldn't have been more thankful for people who lived in Sandcrest longer than her and knew everyone in town.

April's heart raced at the thought of Isaac and Sanchez working together to bring her down. She couldn't believe that she was up against such powerful men. But then again, she had always been a fighter.

She smirked, feeling a sense of satisfaction wash over her. She knew she had the upper hand now. With this new information, she could finally take down Isaac Greenfield and make him pay for what he did to her.

Though they didn't do anything illegal, April was sure that Isaac wouldn't want anyone knowing that he'd been trying to bother a local business. That wouldn't look good in his mayoral campaign.

And now that she had proof that he was trying to take her down, she could show everyone the kind of man he truly was.

***

The sound of her short heels bounced off of the empty walls of town hall. It was later in the day when almost everyone had gone home.

April walked confidently down the hallway, her eyes fixed on the door with Isaac Greenfield's nameplate on it. She had prepared for this moment for hours with her friends' help.

As she reached the door, she took a deep breath, her heart racing with anticipation.

Without knocking, she pushed the door open, revealing Isaac sitting behind his desk, his eyes widening in surprise at the sight of her.

"April, what are you doing here?" he asked, trying to sound calm, but failing miserably.

It was one of her tactics. Catch them off guard.

"I find it funny that you thought I wouldn't figure it out. That you thought I wouldn't do my research and hunt down every little detail about you out there. You underestimated a lawyer. It was a rookie mistake," she said, walking inside and closing the door behind her.

Isaac leaned back in his chair, looking almost amused. "And what exactly did you figure out, April? Did you find my parking ticket from five years ago?"

His smug attitude thrilled her. The cockier he was, the harder he would fall when she took him down.

"Oh, don't play dumb with me, Isaac. I know everything," she said, her voice dripping with confidence. "I know about your little donation to Stay Green and your partnership with councilman Sanchez. You thought you could scare me into shutting down my business, but you messed with the wrong woman."

Isaac's face paled slightly, a flicker of fear passing through his eyes. "I'm not sure what you're talking about," he said, his voice laced with false innocence. "It's public knowledge that I gave to his business. He's an old friend."

"An old friend that would lie for you," April sat down opposite of him and leaned towards his desk. "You gave him that donation so he would try and take me down. That's the only reason you would ever do anything for someone else. You're the most selfish person I've ever had the displeasure of meeting."

Isaac chuckled, his eyes still trying to convey innocence. "I don't know what kind of conspiracy theories you're entertaining, April. But I assure you, I have nothing to do with any of this."

April smirked. "Okay, let's say that you didn't conspire to shut down my business. That doesn't add up to the lies I've been sent from Sanchez's office."

He fiddled with his hands in his lap, looking for a place to put them. For the first time, Isaac seemed off of his game. And April was loving it.

"There has been a misunderstanding," he said finally, his voice barely above a whisper. "Sanchez and I made an agreement that was beneficial to both parties."

"Misunderstanding?" April scoffed. "You mean you lied and manipulated me so you could get away with shutting down my plans?"

When he didn't have anything else to say to that, she continued, "The little threat you sent me about the fake law has his office's name on it. He would be implicated. And I'm willing to bet he would blame it all on you if things were to come out."

Isaac's eyes darted around the room, looking for an escape. But he knew he had none. "What do you want, April?"

"I want you to stop," she said firmly. "And if you don't stop, I'll let the entire island know what you've done to me. They'll see just how far you'll go to get what you want, no matter how ethical it is. And you'll have to kiss your mayoral campaign goodbye."

Isaac sat there, his face contorted with anger and frustration. He knew he had been caught, and there was nothing he could do about it.

He opened his mouth to talk, but April wasn't finished. "I'm going to continue doing what I'm doing, including making plans for a horse ranch on my property. I'm doing everything by the book, legally. And if you come after me, I'll be sure that you're exposed as the liar that you are."

"Fine," he mumbled. "You can have your little horse farm for now. Just know that this isn't over. Whatever you think you've won, you haven't seen the last of me."

April stood up, her eyes blazing with a hint of defiance. "I know exactly what I've won, Isaac. I've won the upper hand, and I'm not afraid to use it. You're just a pathetic man who can't handle a woman who's smarter than him. And I'll be ready for you if you ever decide to cross me again, Isaac."

Isaac didn't say anything, his eyes burning with anger and defeat. She turned around and walked towards the door, feeling like she had just won the battle of her life.

"I'll be back for you, April," he called out before she closed the door to his office.

She didn't need the last word because she'd already won. And she wasn't afraid of him or anything he had to say about it.

As April walked out into the streets of downtown Sandcrest, the air tasted sweeter. The late afternoon sky kissed the horizon perfectly, leaving the clouds to wisp in the wind.

She had finally put Isaac in his place. She had won the game of cat and mouse with Isaac, and she had emerged victorious.

April felt like she had a newfound sense of power within her. She couldn't help but smile as she thought about how she had outsmarted him, how she had taken down a corrupt man who thought he was invincible.

As she walked, she felt a sense of pride wash over her. She had always been a fighter, but this was a new level of accomplishment. She had taken on the most powerful man on the island and come out on top.

For the first time in a long while, she was free. Free from Isaac's threats, free from his lies, and free from his manipulation.

She felt like she could take on the world, and she was ready for whatever came her way. She had no idea what the future held, but she was ready to face it head-on.

Whatever Isaac thought he could do to her now, he was wrong. She would come out stronger, better, smarter.

April felt a rush of adrenaline as she walked down the street, her mind racing with new ideas and endless possibilities. She had always been a woman of ambition, and now she felt unstoppable.

The light breeze carried the scent of the ocean and the sound of seagulls in the distance.

April walked towards the beach, finally get to the shore. She loved the feeling of sand between her toes as she walked along the shoreline. It gave her a sense of freedom that she had never felt before.

The beach waves whispered to her as they lapped onto the shore. It was the same sight she saw every day, but after a conversation like that, she felt renewed.

She decided to walk home and bask in the relaxation she felt as she listened to the sounds of the ocean.

All of her battles had been fought. Or so she thought.

CHAPTER TWENTY SEVEN

April arrived back at her bed and breakfast, ready to face the responsibility again. She was exhausted from the events of the day, but she also felt an inner strength that she hadn't felt before.

She opened the door of her room and was immediately filled with a sense of warmth and comfort. The sun shone through the windows, illuminating every corner of the room.

The bed and breakfast had several guests checking in tomorrow morning, which meant April had a long night of preparing their rooms.

She had to do everything on her own now that Millie was gone. But it was better than having a thief walking around the rooms she so carefully curated.

There were others who could help her in other parts of her life and work. Like Jackson helping with the renovations and ranch. She'll be busy with the bookings, but the others could pick up the slack.

April was determined to make this bed and breakfast a success. She had to remain strong and resilient no matter what came her way.

As she started to work on cleaning the rooms, a part of her felt incomplete. Something wasn't right after everything she accomplished.

Everything had worked out in the end, she thought. But maybe it hadn't. There was something itching at the back of her mind, a feeling she couldn't get rid of. It was a kind of emptiness, as if she needed more closure.

Almost instinctively, she walked out of the room she was cleaning and instead headed right towards the room her father had stayed in.

She hadn't gone in there since he left, but for some reason, she felt like she needed to now. April took a deep breath and turned the doorknob, pushing the door open.

After she told her father to leave the house, she thought maybe he would come to see her again. But he hadn't. He'd left things to sit and fester inside of her.

She wanted him to leave, to figure himself out before coming and asking her to live up to his unreasonable expectations. But she also wanted to make amends, like he said he was here for.

They didn't get many chances to spend that time together like they said they would. And the few chances they did have ended horribly.

Sitting on the bed, she wondered where he could be right now. The island was small, but he could have left already. Would he have had the time and money to book a plane ticket or rent a car?

April couldn't shake the feeling that she needed to find him. She needed closure, and the only way to get it was to talk to him.

She stood up and left the room, determined to find him. She walked out of the bed and breakfast and onto the street, scanning the area for any sign of him. A part of her hoped she would magically remember the exact car he left in, its license plate number, something to identify him.

Then she remembered. When he asked to use her computer, he logged into his email. It was still saved and probably open. Though it wasn't the most ethical, it was the quickest way to find him.

And that's how she was able to find out exactly where her father went.

When she parked at the tiny airport, she wasn't sure if she would make it in time. It was just off the island, but it was nothing like the other airports in the state. Less than a hundred cars were parked outside, which she hoped would work in her favor of finding him.

As April walked into the airport, her heart was pounding in her chest as she scanned the small crowd of people. She knew he was leaving the island, but she didn't know where he was headed.

She only saw the departure time and name of airport in the subject line.

The airport was so small there were only a few gates and a handful of people milling around. It didn't take her long to spot him, just like she thought.

He was sitting at a small coffee shop, sipping on a cup of coffee and reading a newspaper.

April made her way over to him, trying to keep her breathing steady. She didn't want to start the conversation with anger or disappointment.

Her heart leaped with joy and relief. Just as she approached, her father looked up and saw her. Slowly, he set down his newspaper and April to meet her.

"What are you doing here?" he asked, brows furrowed. "How did you know I was here?"

"Email," April replied. "I'm sorry. I just needed to see you before you left."

April should have guessed before that he was leaving her again. It was what he did when things got hard. He came to remind her that she had a father, and then he left again to remind her that he wasn't that good at being one.

They sat down at the coffee shop, and April ordered a cup of tea. For a moment, they sat in silence, neither of them quite sure what to say. Then, her father spoke up.

"I overheard what you said about Georgia's tuition."

It was a strange place to start, but April wasn't surprised he was bringing up her downfalls as a mother. "I have the money somewhere, I was just planning to use it for something else. I'm going to"

Richard interrupted her. "I paid the tuition for the semester."

April's eyes widened in surprise. She couldn't believe what she was hearing. Her father had paid for Georgia's tuition? She didn't know what to say. It was a kind gesture she'd never seen in him before.

"How did you-"

Again, her father spoke up, explaining before she had the chance to ask. "I have money saved up. I know you all think that I'm broke and struggling, but I do have a little nest egg. It's usually just for my travels, but I knew that you needed it more than my trip to Thailand."

Tears pricked the corners of her eyes. To have thousands of dollars off of her back, it was a miracle she didn't deserve.

"Why?" she asked, still in shock.

Her father took a deep breath. "Because I know how hard it is to be afraid of money. And I know I haven't always been there for you, but I wanted to do something to help. It doesn't make up for what I've done. I'm still a screw up and I know that. But I knew it was the right thing to do."

April felt a glimmer of hope. Maybe her father was trying to make amends for all the times he had let her down.

She took a sip of her tea, her mind racing. She had so many questions for him, but she didn't want to scare him off. She knew how easily he could slip away and disappear.

"Thank you," April said quietly, still in shock.

Richard nodded, a small smile on his face. "You're welcome."

She looked at him with new eyes, no longer seeing just the man who had abandoned her time and time again, but also the man who had the capacity for kindness and generosity.

He was right, it didn't make up for everything he'd done. But it was a start. It was proof that her father could do the right thing if given enough chances.

As they finished their drinks, April knew that this moment wouldn't last forever. Her father would leave again, and she would be left to pick up the pieces. But for now, she would savor this moment and hold onto the hope that maybe, just maybe, her father would continue to try to make things right.

April sat there, unsure of what to say next. She wanted to ask him so many questions about his life, what he had been doing, where he had been. But she didn't want to push him away. She would say anything to make this moment last a lifetime.

"I have to go," Richard said, standing up from the table. "My flight is boarding soon."

She opened her mouth, but no words came out. After some thought, she took a deep breath and said, "I forgive you."

Richard's eyes widened in surprise. "What?"

"I want you to know that I forgive you for taking advantage of me and all of the requests at the bed and breakfast. I forgive you. I can't hold onto that anger anymore."

It felt good for the words to fall from her lips. It was the first time she said it to her father. The simple idea of letting go of what he'd done made her chest feel lighter.

April continued, "You've made a lot of mistakes. You've hurt me more times than I can count. But this trip? The trip to the island where you asked for firmer pillows and I blamed you for stealing. This trip I forgive you for."

Richard's eyes glistened with tears as he reached across the table to take April's hand. "Thank you," he said, his voice barely above a whisper. "I don't deserve your forgiveness, but I'm grateful for it nonetheless."

April smiled, feeling a sense of relief wash over her. It was as if a heavy weight had been lifted from her chest. For years, she had carried the burden of her father's mistakes, but now she was finally learning to let go.

He leaned down and kissed her on the forehead before turning to leave. As he walked away, April watched him go, feeling a sense of sadness wash over her.

She didn't know when she would see him again, but she knew that she had done the right thing by forgiving him. It was good for the both of them.

Richard stood by his gate with his suitcase in hand. "I'm sorry it wasn't more fun to see me." He let out a chuckle.

"It wasn't that fun, but I do hope to see you again sometime," April responded with a smile.

Her father smiled before turning and walking down the catwalk to his plane. She waited there until it took off, listening to the loud hum of the engine.

April sat there for a few more minutes, lost in thought. She thought about what had just happened and how far she had come in forgiving her father. She knew that it wasn't going to be easy, but she was finally ready to let go of the past and move forward.

As much as she wanted him to stay and heal her hurt, she knew that it was better to let him go. To let him live his life and not try to control him. She had spent too many years trying to control his actions and his whereabouts. It was time to let go of that need for control and just let him be.

April stood up from the table, taking one last look at the spot where her father had sat just moments before. She smiled to herself, feeling a sense of peace that she'd finally gotten closure.

The air was cool as she walked back out to her car. The sky was turning dark, and she wished she had brought an extra sweatshirt with her.

After everything she'd done, working hard to solve all of her problems the best she could, she finally felt satisfied.

EPILOGUE

Nigel's hand brushed her arm as he set down the plates in front of her. He'd made a beautiful dinner for them both. It was a date to make up for the one that was ruined by Lily's appearance.

April looked up at him, feeling grateful for his presence in her life. Nigel had been there for her through it all, supporting her as she struggled to come to terms with everything she'd been through the past week.

"Thank you for this," she said, smiling up at him. "It looks delicious."

Nigel leaned over and kissed her on the cheek. "Anything for you," he said, his voice soft and gentle.

April felt a wave of affection wash over her. Nigel was kind, loving, and everything she had ever wanted in a partner. She knew that she was lucky to have him in her life. She was lucky that he chose her in the end.

The table was adorned with white linens and centered by an elegant arrangement of candles and flowers. Silverware was arranged neatly around two settings.

The warm light of the candles gave everything on the table a pleasant glow. Matched with the sunset, the ambiance was beautifully set up for a romantic evening.

As they took their first bites, April felt a sense of contentment wash over her. "Oh man," she said, mouth full of tortellini. "This is excellent."

The scent of delicious food filled the air, a blend of herbs and spices that tantalized the senses. A hint of floral and sweet scents wafted from the centerpieces to provide a pleasant undertone.

Nigel's fork squeaked across his plate as he scraped up the pasta. "Thank you! I tried hard on these ones. This is make-up tortellini. Because this is a make-up date."

April chuckled. "Well, it's definitely making up for everything that's happened this past week."

They continued eating in comfortable silence, enjoying the taste of the delicious meal and each other's company. April couldn't help but feel grateful for the life she had built for herself. Despite all the challenges she had faced, she had come out the other side stronger and happier.

"You look gorgeous tonight," Nigel said, eyeing her up and down. She loved when his eyes wandered.

April felt a blush spread across her cheeks as Nigel's gaze lingered on her. She wore a simple black dress that hugged her curves in all the right places. Her hair was pulled back in a messy bun, with a few strands framing her face. She felt confident and beautiful, and Nigel's compliment only added to her joy.

"Thank you, you look quite handsome yourself," she replied, taking a sip of her wine.

Nigel grinned, his eyes sparkling in the candlelight. "Well, I had to look good for you. You're hard to impress."

"Is that what you think of me?" she asked with a wide-mouthed smile, almost offended by the comment. "That I'm hard to impress?"

"You are!" he cried out. They laughed together, filling the room with sounds of their enjoyment.

After they died down, he explained, "You have high standards. It's actually a good thing. It means that you vet the people in your life. I'm honored to be the one on this date tonight because I know you demand and deserved the best."

She was honored by his words. It was like he always knew exactly what to say and when to say it.

April felt a sense of warmth settle over her as she looked at Nigel. He was right, she did have high standards, and he had met every single one of them.

"I'm glad you think so highly of me," she said, her voice barely above a whisper.

Nigel reached a hand over and squeezed hers. "Of course I do. You're amazing, April. I'm lucky to have you in my life."

A smile tugged at the corners of her mouth. "I feel the same way."

The rest of the evening passed in a blur of laughter. Their conversation flowed effortlessly as they ate, discussing everything from work to their future plans. Nigel was a good listener, always attentive and supportive of her dreams.

As the night drew to a close, Nigel stood up from the table and took April's hand in his. He kissed her deeply, lingering on her lips for as long as possible.

April's heart raced as they pulled away from each other. Nigel's eyes sparkled with desire as he looked at her, making her feel like the only woman in the world.

Without a word, he took her hand and led her out onto the balcony. The stars were shining brightly in the sky, casting a romantic glow over everything. Nigel stood behind her, wrapping his arms around her waist and holding her close.

April leaned back into him, feeling his warmth and strength. She turned her head to look at him, and he leaned down to kiss her again, softly.

This time, they were interrupted by a soft buzz coming from April's pocket. Who would be calling her at a time as special as this?

"Why don't you get that and I'll clean up from dinner," Nigel suggested, still inches away from her face. She could feel his breath hot on her face and didn't want to pull away.

But she knew she probably had to. What if it was Georgia or some emergency at the bed and breakfast? "Alright, fine. But I'll be back in as soon as I'm done."

"Deal," Nigel said, raising his brows before walking into the apartment, shutting the sliding door to the balcony behind him.

April immediately felt a chill come behind her where Nigel's warm body was just seconds before. Whatever this was, it had better be important.

Alice's name popped up on her screen, and she accepted the call. "Hey, Alice, what's going on? Everything okay?"

"April, we have new information. Hold on, let me put you on speaker," she said, followed by shuffles from her setting down the phone and pushing buttons.

There was a loud echo of greetings as April recognized Beth, Alice and Kellie on the line.

"What's going on?" April asked, her heart racing with anticipation. She couldn't help but wonder what new information they had that felt like it couldn't wait.

"Kellie and I," Beth began, "were at the diner and we overheard a few people talking... It sounded like-"

"I think it was two of the Harrisons and a few of the people from the outskirts of the island, like over by seventh? Do you know that crowd?" Kellie interrupted, giving no details that could help April figure out what was happening.

"Anyway," Beth continued, clearly frustrated with the intrusion. "It sounded like Isaac Greenfield is getting some traction with people who like his ideas."

April's heart sank. She was hoping that after her threats, he would be doing worse in the polls.

But this wasn't just about his mayoral campaign. There was something else going on. All four of them knew that he would have some supporters.

There must have been something else happening. Something they were afraid to tell her.

"What kind of traction?" April asked, trying to keep the fear out of her voice.

"They were talking about him like he's some kind of savior. Like he's going to save the island from all its problems," Alice chimed in.

April felt a knot form in her stomach. This didn't sound good. "What else did you hear? What's got you all riled up?"

Everyone was quiet for longer than it felt comfortable.

"Remember that bill he was trying to make law? The one about not having any more horses on the island?" Beth asked.

"Right. That was supposed to be part of his campaign. But no one would go for that. The horses are a historic part of the island. Everyone loves them," April tried to explain. "Right?"

"That's the thing, April," Kellie chimed in. "It seems like people are starting to buy into his propaganda. People are interested in what he has to say. They were talking about getting rid of the horses. People are approving of his idea."

April felt her heartbreak at the news. The horses were one of the things that made the island special. She couldn't imagine the town getting rid of them. And yet, here they were agreeing with the guy who wanted to displace them all.

"April? Are you okay?" she heard Alice's voice say.

"Yeah, yes," she said, snapping back into the conversation. "We'll just have to fight harder. We've gotten him before, we'll get him again."

"Right," Kellie said. "We can do this."

The ladies said goodbye and hung up the phone, leaving April with her thoughts.

Isaac Greenfield said he would be back to try and beat her again. If it was a war he wanted, that's exactly what he would get.

The nerve of Isaac to try and take away the island's historic charm. The horses were a part of the island's identity, something that couldn't be replaced. And yet, people were starting to believe in his propaganda. It was up to her to make sure that didn't happen.

April knew this time it would be different. Because she wasn't by herself, she had people to support her. This time, she would have more allies, more help, more friends.

When Isaac Greenfield was ready to fight, April would be stronger than ever.

NOW AVAILABLE!

A CHANCE ROMANCE
(The Inn at Dune Island—Book 3)

In this new romantic comedy series by #1 Bestseller Fiona Grace, life gets turned upside down for April Faith when her daughter leaves for college, her corporate job jades her, and her husband abruptly walks out. April realizes she has lived life too long for others, and she needs a major change. She remembers Dune Island, her childhood summer home off the coast of Georgia, a place where nothing could go wrong in the world—and she needs to revisit what remains of her family's historic beach house and see if she can restore it, turn it into an inn, open the door for a new life—and maybe, even, a new love...

"Wow, this book takes off & never stops! I couldn't put it down! Highly recommended for those who love a great mystery with twists, turns, romance, and a long lost family member! I am reading the next book right now!"
--Amazon reviewer (regarding *Murder in the Manor*)

"Wish all books were this good a mystery romance and love. Did not want to stop reading this book—loved it."
--Amazon reviewer (regarding *Murder in the Manor*)

A CHANCE ROMANCE is book #3 in a new romance series by #1 bestselling author Fiona Grace, whose books have received over 10,000 five-star reviews and ratings.

A sweet romance series filled with twists at every turn, THE INN AT DUNE ISLAND will make you laugh and cry as it transports you to a magical place. A page-turner packed with jaw-dropping twists, impossible to put down, it will make you fall in love with romance all over again.

Future books in the series are also available!

"The story line wasn't just a who done it, but had a story about her life and romance, including village life. Very entertaining."
--Amazon reviewer (regarding *Murder in the Manor*)

"It has endearing and sometimes quirky characters, a plot that keeps you reading and the right amount of romance. I can't wait to start book two!"
--Amazon reviewer (regarding *Murder in the Manor*)

"What a great story of murder, romance, new beginnings, love, friend ships and a wonderful cascade of mystery."
--Amazon reviewer (regarding *Murder in the Manor*)

Fiona Grace

Fiona Grace is author of the LACEY DOYLE COZY MYSTERY series, comprising nine books; of the TUSCAN VINEYARD COZY MYSTERY series, comprising seven books; of the DUBIOUS WITCH COZY MYSTERY series, comprising three books; of the BEACHFRONT BAKERY COZY MYSTERY series, comprising six books; of the CATS AND DOGS COZY MYSTERY series, comprising nine books; of the ELIZA MONTAGU COZY MYSTERY series, comprising nine books (and counting); of the ENDLESS HARBOR ROMANTIC COMEDY series, comprising nine books (and counting); of the INN AT DUNE ISLAND ROMANTIC COMEDY series, comprising five books (and counting); of the INN BY THE SEA ROMANTIC COMEDY series, comprising five books (and counting); and of the MAID AND THE MANSION COZY MYSTERY series, comprising five books (and counting).

Fiona would love to hear from you, so please visit www.fionagraceauthor.com to receive free ebooks, hear the latest news, and stay in touch.

A FLAPPER FATALITY (Book #5)
BUMPED BY A DAME (Book #6)
A DOLL'S DEBACLE (Book #7)
A FELLA'S RUIN (Book #8)
A GAL'S OFFING (Book #9)

LACEY DOYLE COZY MYSTERY
MURDER IN THE MANOR (Book#1)
DEATH AND A DOG (Book #2)
CRIME IN THE CAFE (Book #3)
VEXED ON A VISIT (Book #4)
KILLED WITH A KISS (Book #5)
PERISHED BY A PAINTING (Book #6)
SILENCED BY A SPELL (Book #7)
FRAMED BY A FORGERY (Book #8)
CATASTROPHE IN A CLOISTER (Book #9)

TUSCAN VINEYARD COZY MYSTERY
AGED FOR MURDER (Book #1)
AGED FOR DEATH (Book #2)
AGED FOR MAYHEM (Book #3)
AGED FOR SEDUCTION (Book #4)
AGED FOR VENGEANCE (Book #5)
AGED FOR ACRIMONY (Book #6)
AGED FOR MALICE (Book #7)

DUBIOUS WITCH COZY MYSTERY
SKEPTIC IN SALEM: AN EPISODE OF MURDER (Book #1)
SKEPTIC IN SALEM: AN EPISODE OF CRIME (Book #2)
SKEPTIC IN SALEM: AN EPISODE OF DEATH (Book #3)

BEACHFRONT BAKERY COZY MYSTERY
BEACHFRONT BAKERY: A KILLER CUPCAKE (Book #1)
BEACHFRONT BAKERY: A MURDEROUS MACARON (Book #2)
BEACHFRONT BAKERY: A PERILOUS CAKE POP (Book #3)
BEACHFRONT BAKERY: A DEADLY DANISH (Book #4)
BEACHFRONT BAKERY: A TREACHEROUS TART (Book #5)
BEACHFRONT BAKERY: A CALAMITOUS COOKIE (Book #6)

CATS AND DOGS COZY MYSTERY

A VILLA IN SICILY: OLIVE OIL AND MURDER (Book #1)
A VILLA IN SICILY: FIGS AND A CADAVER (Book #2)
A VILLA IN SICILY: VINO AND DEATH (Book #3)
A VILLA IN SICILY: CAPERS AND CALAMITY (Book #4)
A VILLA IN SICILY: ORANGE GROVES AND VENGEANCE
(Book #5)
A VILLA IN SICILY: CANNOLI AND A CASUALTY (Book #6)

Made in the USA
Las Vegas, NV
01 April 2024

88098401R00090